"You're such a pal, Lauren."

A pal. She was a pal. P-A-L—which could stand for Pitiful Always Around.

Lauren controlled the sudden raw anger that consumed her. The man in front of her probably didn't even have a clue that she was interested in advancing their relationship. She was like a properly functioning computer—taken for granted and low maintenance.

At twenty-eight she didn't want to be a pal any longer. She wanted to be the girlfriend. Wanted to be the hot sexy one he couldn't refuse or resist. While her biological clock wasn't exactly ticking—okay, maybe a little—she did want the whole shebang: marriage, career and family.

She'd waited long enough for Mr. Secure and Safe to notice her. She'd have to be the one to make a move....

Dear Reader,

One of my favorite short stories is O. Henry's
"The Gift of the Magi," the story of a married couple
who each sell their most valuable personal possessions
so they can buy the other a worthy present. Although
at first the Christmas gifts they purchase for each other
seem useless and foolish, the reader learns that true
wisdom is putting others' needs and desires before
one's own, and this path leads to the truest love.

For Justin Wright, the girl who's been haunting his dreams
ever since a very seductive dance just before Christmas is
his co-worker Lauren Brown. Unfortunately, she doesn't
want him in her stocking. Instead, she thinks she wants
Jeff, Justin's identical twin and the man the dance was
intended for. What's chivalrous Justin to do? Be Lauren's
hero, of course; show her what real love is all about
and show her that *he's* her Mr. Wright, not only for
the holidays, but for ever.

I hope you enjoy Lauren and Justin's quest for love as
much as I did writing about it. O. Henry wrote his story in
an afternoon; mine took a little longer. May your holidays
be filled with joy and happiness—and enjoy the romance.

Best wishes!

Michele Dunaway

Books by Michele Dunaway

HARLEQUIN AMERICAN ROMANCE

UNWRAPPING MR. WRIGHT
Michele Dunaway

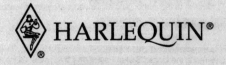

HARLEQUIN®

TORONTO • NEW YORK • LONDON
AMSTERDAM • PARIS • SYDNEY • HAMBURG
STOCKHOLM • ATHENS • TOKYO • MILAN • MADRID
PRAGUE • WARSAW • BUDAPEST • AUCKLAND

ISBN 0-373-75048-X

UNWRAPPING MR. WRIGHT

Copyright © 2004 by Michele Dunaway.

To all my friends at eHarlequin.com,
and to Trish Gazall, Ken Williams and Vic Porcelli
at FM 101.1 The River. Thanks.

And always, to Jon for believing in me.

Chapter One

Justin Wright was Scrooge.

Not that he looked anything like good old Ebenezer. He was too young and too good-looking for that. "Hot," some misguided temp had called him. But that didn't stop the modern-day tightwad from frowning, leaning over the conference table and saying to Lauren Brown, current object of his wrath, "You know, in all my time in this company, this has to be the dumbest way to spend money that I've ever heard."

Lauren twirled the red-and-white candy-cane pen between her fingers, but the motion did little to calm her or fill her with any of her usual boisterous Christmas spirit. It did, however, keep her from reaching across and strangling the annoying, self-centered Justin Wright. At this moment, the fact that he was her boss was irrelevant.

He tapped his fingers on the table, creating an annoying staccato. "You know, Lauren, the more I think about it, the more I have to disagree. That idea is a waste of money. My company's. We hired you for this?"

Justin Wright squared his chin stubbornly, but Lauren Brown glared right back at him. Her icy brown stare, though, like the rest of her, went totally unnoticed by the man who, unfortunately, looked too much like his gorgeous twin. Lauren tried thinning her lips in displeasure, but that, too, had little impact on her nemesis.

Once again she exhaled slowly in an attempt to rein in her temper. In the six months that she'd been working for Wright Solutions, nothing she'd proposed had been good enough for the high standards of the ultra-picky, master micromanager Justin Wright. She set down the pen down lest she use it as a dagger.

"As a matter of fact, you did hire me for this," she said in a sweet tone that still contained an edge of steel. "You hired me for PR, and that's exactly what the office Christmas party is. That's why Jared, president of this company, assigned me the job of hosting it and that's why we're having it at a hotel, two weekends from now, on December 18."

The way Justin's lips turned down indicated he hadn't liked her noting that his elder brother was president. "But semiformal to formal? You've already got an open bar. What's wrong with nachos and beer after hours? That's worked ever since we started this company. Now we're wining and dining employees with filet mignon and champagne?"

She stared right into his eyes, trying to hold her own against the glittering green. "Yes, we are."

"Jared shouldn't have given you free rein."

She shrugged. "Then it's lucky for me that he did, isn't it? Nachos and beer out, filet mignon and champagne in." She left out the "deal with it," although from his scowl he'd heard her unspoken challenge. "As president, Jared left me in complete control as long as I don't overspend my budget, which I haven't. You don't need to worry during your interim stay while he's on his honeymoon."

Lauren grabbed her candy-cane pen and doodled a small red smiley face before scratching out the happy symbol. If only Jared were back! Unlike Justin, the eldest of the three Wright sons had a vision for the company. Too bad he'd extended his honeymoon by another four weeks. He and his new wife weren't returning to St. Louis until early in the new year.

Justin's only vision was girls in tight skirts and fishnet panty hose. Unfortunately, the playboy of the family had endless charm, and with the number of women Lauren had seen flocking around, she knew that he knew it. However, at twenty-eight, Lauren prided herself on the fact that she knew better. She'd known Justin for three years and she was proud that she remained singularly unimpressed and unaffected by anything he did or said.

"You did hear me, didn't you?"

She blinked and glanced over at him. See how unaffected she was? She hadn't even heard a word he'd been saying. Knowing Justin, though, she took a stab and gave him a classic PR answer. "I heard you," Lauren replied, "and I thank you for your opinion."

She tactfully omitted the word *unwelcome,* but as if sensing it anyway, Justin narrowed his eyes sharply. Lauren set the merry little pen down. "But as this is my area of expertise, I must respectfully disagree with your assessment of everything." To avoid Justin's obvious displeasure, Lauren looked for support to Clint Seaver, her immediate boss and the vice president of Public Relations and Marketing. He had a silly grin on his face, as if watching Justin and Lauren spar was more exciting than the St. Louis Blues hockey games he loved.

"I was hired to make Wright Solutions a prominent player, with growth like that of Microsoft in the 1990s. To do this, Wright Solutions needs to do many things besides the Christmas party. Next year I plan to—"

"Whatever. As you said, Jared gave you control of the Christmas party. Just don't overspend your budget or you'll answer to me." Justin had cut her off as though the conversation had suddenly become irrelevant and now bored him. Lauren's jaw dropped at his boorishness, though she quickly recovered and closed her mouth. Never had the despicable Mr. Wright been this rude.

This time, though, he didn't look at her again or explain his actions. He glanced at his watch and turned his attention to Clint. "It's your budget for next year, Clint. If you think including the projects Lauren is about to tell me about—again—is the way to go, fine. Let her run with them. I'll expect a full report on my desk in two weeks regarding your plans for the new year. Before I go, are we still on for poker tonight?"

Clint grinned, the grin of someone secure about being in the inner circle, the grin of someone who had been friends with the three Wright brothers ever since high school. "Me miss a Friday-night poker bash? Never. We're definitely on. My place tonight."

"Super. I'll see you at seven." With that, Justin Wright stood and, without another word or glance in Lauren's direction, left the conference room.

Good riddance, Lauren thought as he disappeared from sight. Never had she met a man so temperamentally different from his brothers.

Justin's elder brother, Jared, was kind and gentle, yet steely and strong. Justin's twin, Jeff, was puppy-dog adorable, the type of guy that a girl just wanted to hug and take care of. He was safe, predictable, the kind of man a girl looked for after being burned once too often by Mr. Wrong. It didn't hurt that he wasn't bad looking, either. Not as hot or handsome as his twin brother— few men were like Justin Wright—but Jeff was near enough. And he didn't have Justin's attitude, which made Jeff a much better catch.

Lauren knew how safe and wonderful Jeff was because she had lived next to him for the past three years. Her condo shared a wall with Jeff's and he'd been the one to tell her about the new position at Wright Solutions that his twin had reluctantly created.

Of course, if from the beginning Lauren had realized she would be working this closely with the condescending womanizer, she might not have even considered the job. She picked up her pad of paper, her candy-cane pen and, after everyone else preceded her, left the conference room.

Oh, who was she kidding? Even she had to admit that despite Justin Wright, this job was perfect for her talents and her media communications degree from Webster University.

Instead of being one of twenty PR specialists doing mindless press releases and endless corporate brochures the way she had been at Simons and Simmons Public Relations, here at Wright Solutions she had the chance to really make a difference. She was a hometown girl and she could grow with a hometown company.

Clint aside, Lauren *was* the PR department, and the future and her private stock options had an unlimited ceiling. And then there was the best perk of all—working with Jeff Wright, man of her dreams. Jeff was the company's first responder to any computer or software crisis. She made a quick stop in the copy room, picked up a stack of file folders and walked to her small office, with its lovely view of the parking lot and the building next door.

Speak of the devil.

"So how'd it go?" Jeff leaned against her doorjamb. He and Justin were easy to tell apart once you got to know them: Jeff had a softer face, different from the harder edged face that made girls swoon over his twin. Jeff's chin rounded more than Justin's more square one, and Jeff's Roman nose was crooked from being broken in a long-ago hockey game. Although they both had green eyes, Justin's were a dark emerald shade, whereas Jeff's were the color of light green cellophane.

Lauren flashed Jeff her best dazzling smile. "Great."

"Super," Jeff said. He didn't notice or mention her fitted red Christmas sweater, which she'd worn just for him. "Hopefully, it wasn't too bad. Justin really is taking this running-the-show stuff seriously while Jared's gone. Hey, I'm going to be working late tonight and I need a favor. Could you iron my blue pinstripe?"

Lauren's gut clenched, but she covered her reaction by simply raising an eyebrow. "Have a date?"

Jeff grinned and Lauren's heart softened. She recognized *that* grin. "Sort of. Tomorrow night's Mom's birthday. We're taking her out to Tony's to celebrate."

"All of you? Tony's is fancy. Suit coat, tie—the works. You're sure?"

Jeff nodded. "Yeah, well, it is for Mom. And it'll be all of us except for Jared. You know, I don't get my older brother. Who would go on a honeymoon for a month and then extend it by another four weeks?"

"I would if I found the right man," Lauren said. "Sun, surf and…" She left the word *sex* unsaid.

Jeff arched a strawberry-blond eyebrow at her. In Lauren's opinion, Jeff had the most handsome shade of red hair—not too red, nor too orangy blond. It was simply perfect. With his twinkling green eyes, he'd won a St. Patrick's Day "dress as a leprechaun" contest once. That Justin's hair was the same gorgeous color was irrelevant.

"Yeah, I guess you girls would want to keep a guy out of commission that long. It wouldn't be so bad if I could bring my laptop, but Jared doesn't even turn his on every day. Like I said, I just don't get him." Jeff shrugged his broad shoulders for emphasis, indicating exactly how foolish he thought his madly-in-love elder brother was.

"Anyway, just grab the shirt—you know the one— out of my closet. I've got some software to finish writing and I doubt I'll even make it home until well past midnight."

Lauren adored that Jeff was such a committed computer geek. Not that he looked or acted like it, but given a choice of dating or programming, the computer won hands down every time. Jeff always maintained that computers were a lot simpler to deal with than women. Justin, however, was the opposite.

"Want me to leave you some dinner?" she asked. "Something to microwave? I'll put it in your refrigerator when I return your shirt."

Jeff gave her an appreciative smile. "That would be great. You know I always forget to eat when I get caught up in work. What would I do without you? You're such a pal, Lauren." He shifted, and she could tell he itched to return to his computer and the program he was writing. "I'll catch you later, okay?"

"Sure," Lauren said. She watched a whistling Jeff walk away until he disappeared around a corner. Unlike his annoying brother, Jeff Wright was a dream. In the past three years, he'd become her best friend. They talked constantly and shared things like chores and food. She sighed suddenly and plucked a fuzzy piece of red lint off her sweater. Everyone in the office said red was her color, but Jeff hadn't even noticed.

She frowned as a sense of disquiet came over her. After three years, one would have expected a little more from their relationship. It should have changed somehow, some way. They were friends; they got along great; they'd each been burned once or twice. That made them perfect for each other—they'd have the kind of relationship based on mutual respect, with some love and attention thrown in.

Except that the love and attention were still sadly lacking.

Right then and there she decided that Jeff Wright needed to notice her, really notice her. Couldn't he see how perfect they'd be together?

But then, Jeff Wright was often a man with blinders

on. When he focused on a computer problem he could be so one-tracked that he would forget to eat. Not once, though, had he made any type of move on her. He'd always treated her chivalrously, as if she was a treasured friend. His cryptic words suddenly resounded in her ears: "You're such a pal, Lauren."

A pal. She was a pal. P-A-L, which could stand for Pitiful Always-Around Lauren. Lauren controlled the sudden raw anger that consumed her. Jeff probably didn't even have a clue that she was interested in taking their relationship further. She was like a properly functioning computer—taken for granted and low maintenance.

At twenty-eight, she didn't want to be Jeff's pal any longer. She wanted to be the girlfriend! Wanted to be the hot sexy one he couldn't refuse or resist. While her biological clock wasn't exactly ticking—okay, maybe a little—she did want the whole shebang: marriage, career and family.

She wanted Jeff Wright. She didn't know if they'd have any chemistry, but who cared? She'd been there, done that. Passion flared and burned out. It was stability she craved now in a twosome, and that was Jeff. She'd waited long enough for Mr. Secure and Safe to notice her. She'd have to be the one to make a move.

"Do you always hang out in doorways?" Justin Wright appeared in the hall between her office and the cubicles in the center of the building; a dubious look on his face. Just how long had he been there? He glanced upward as he inched toward the opposite wall. "Well, not that. I don't see any mistletoe."

Did he think she was that desperate? "I'm being creative," she retorted—the first reply that came to her lips. "And, yes, you pay me for that." She heard him laugh as she entered her office and shut the door behind her decisively.

Lauren tossed the file folders onto her desk. The candy-cane pen fell to the floor. Jeff's words again rang in her ears, this time louder than the church bells on Christmas morning. *You're a pal, Lauren. A pal.*

Oh, how she hated that phrase. Just how many times had she heard those exact words or their variation in the years since high school? How many times had she been told, "You're a great friend, Lauren, but I just don't want you the way I want—" Every guy said the same thing; the only thing that changed was the girl's name. And the one man who hadn't—he was still a lesson in heartache that she never wanted to repeat.

Lauren stomped her foot with newfound determination. She sat down in her overstuffed desk chair and reached into the desk drawer. Her fingers fished in her purse for the mirror she knew she had but rarely used. Moving it at various angles, she took stock of herself. Brown hair. Brown eyes. Boring makeup. Practical business attire except for the red sweater. All told, nothing to write home about. The woman she could only see in bits and pieces in the looking glass was not a girl for a guy to get excited about.

And to hook Jeff Wright, she had to get him excited. She'd seen him with a few bimbos over the years. The relationships never lasted long, maybe a week or two before his interest waned or they tired of his job coming first.

Most of his women had one thing in common: they were blond. Insight hit her. Maybe that was what she needed. Hair color. Tweezed eyebrows. Pouty red lips. Those things certainly couldn't hurt. Beauty and brains in one sexy, irresistible package. Perhaps if she just spiced up the package—like spicing up a résumé or making a computer run faster—she could catch Jeff Wright.

The Yellow Pages thumped open as Lauren flipped to the beauty parlor listings. She ran her finger down the black print, her gaze searching for the day-spa salon that did all those makeovers for the local news channel. The door to her office opened.

Lauren's head shot up and she quickly closed the phone book, keeping her arm inside it to hold her place. In this position she was bent over at an ungodly angle, her right hip jutting out. "Yes?"

"You seemed upset about something earlier," Justin said as he entered her office. "I thought I'd stop in and see if I'd offended you in some way, or at least more than I usually do. If I did, I want to apologize. I haven't caught you at a bad time, have I?"

Lauren shifted a little, covering any telltale clues that might reveal her makeover goals. "Uh, no. And no, I'm not upset at all," Lauren replied. She added a wide smile to make her lie convincing. Hopefully, he'd get a clue and leave. Justin cocked his head. He didn't look too persuaded and he made no move to go back out the door.

She knew how silly she must appear with her arm stuck in a phone book and her rear end sticking up. Her face flushed as it heated under Justin's appraising stare. "Um, apology accepted, not that there was a need," she added to the lie—anything to get him out of her office.

"Did you have anything else?" she asked.

"Yeah," Justin said slowly. Lauren's arm started to numb and she again shifted under his intent appraisal. "I'd just realized that I didn't tell you I had an overseas call scheduled, which is why I left the meeting so abruptly. I didn't want you to think I was being rude when I cut you off in the conference room today."

He was worried about being rude? Please. After six months of working with him, it was a little too late for worrying about that. The man defined *rude*. Lauren struggled to stop herself from laughing at the bitter irony. She managed to keep her tone sarcasm-free as she said, "No problem. Our constant sparring keeps my job interesting. Honestly."

"If you're sure." Justin walked over toward her desk, and Lauren inched the Yellow Pages closer to her body. He frowned. "That's a great sweater on you. By the way, what are you doing?"

Surely he wasn't picking this very moment to start

being civil by chitchatting with her. "I have an important call to make." She glanced pointedly at the phone book. "I don't want to lose my place."

"Oh." He tempered his curiosity and gave her a charming smile. Despite her previous imperviousness to him, Lauren flushed more, this time not because she was in an ungraceful position.

No wonder women liked Justin. Even she now had to admit that she wasn't totally immune to his killer I'll-melt-that-heart-of-yours grin. Seeing she wasn't about to elaborate on the details of her phone call, Justin said, "Well, okay, then. I guess I should tell you to have a good weekend and get out of your way."

Lauren nodded. "You have a good weekend, too." She watched him leave, and tried to look pleasant when he stopped at the door and turned back around.

"Lauren?" he said.

"Yes?"

"We do have Post-It notes in the supply closet. You know, to hold your place," he added, and with that he left. She swore she heard him laughing as he closed her door behind him.

She counted to twenty just to make sure he wouldn't return, and then she sat down and reopened the phone book. She ran her finger down the page and found the number she was looking for. It was time Lauren "before" became Lauren "after," a femme fatale.

She secured an appointment for Monday, and composed e-mails to Justin and Clint indicating that she was taking a personal day. She frowned as she hit Send. Justin Wright. So different from his brother. He raised every one of her hackles. He had that lethal smile that needed to be outlawed. He…ooh. Jeff was definitely the better of the two men. Definitely.

Satisfaction filled her as she leaned back against the plush leather desk chair. Jeff loved *Monday Night Football*. They often watched it together, sharing beer and popcorn. But if she had her way—and oh, would she— Jeff Wright wasn't going to do much football watching this Monday night. Instead, they were going to play. Yes, come December 6, the better of the two men was in for a very big holiday surprise.

Chapter Two

Justin Wright tossed the briefcase down. It landed on his desk with an annoying thump. Mondays should be outlawed, especially Mondays following your mother's birthday party. "Sylvia!"

"Yes?" His secretary of the past five years poked her head in through the open doorway.

"Where's Lauren? Didn't you call for her as I asked you to?"

Familiar with his many moods, Sylvia backed up slightly. "She's not in today."

That didn't sound good. Perhaps he'd misunderstood his secretary. Frustration had him speaking a bit slower. "What do you mean, she's not in today? Is she late? At a meeting?"

Sylvia inched another step backward as if she were afraid he'd massacre the messenger. "No. She's not coming in at all. She took a personal day. The details are in her e-mail to you. She sent me a copy. I'm surprised you didn't see it. Don't you always check your work e-mails on the weekend?"

Patience was a virtue that he always found himself short of on Mondays. He followed the retreating Sylvia to her desk. "I didn't check my work e-mail this weekend. My floors are all torn up, my house is a disaster, and that meant I had to move my computer into storage. Jeff still hasn't fixed the glitch in my laptop. Plus, I had my mother's birthday party to attend."

Sylvia brightened. She and Mrs. Wright had chatted for ages when Mrs. Wright dropped by the office to check on her three sons. "Oh, how was that? Did you have a lovely dinner?"

"It was great," Justin said. Well, it had been if he didn't count his mother harping on her two youngest boys to find women and settle down like their beloved older brother. "After all, you *are* thirty," his mother had reminded both of them at least ten times. She'd also made those remarks about wanting to see grandchildren before she died. Reminding her she was only fifty-five hadn't helped. Justin sincerely hoped Jared's wife came back pregnant. It might alleviate one crisis: getting his mother off his case. "Is Clint available?"

Sylvia sat behind her desk. "No. Remember? He's at that luncheon in Springfield with the representatives from Kramer and McGee."

A creature of having his space perfect, Justin decided the weekend must have thrown him even more than he'd realized; he'd forgotten that. "Wonderful. And Lauren decided to up and take a personal day. Couldn't she have told me Friday?"

Frustrated, he threw a hand into the air. What was the point in having a public relations director if she didn't work? Okay, so she hadn't missed a day in six months. But today the company had not one but two major crises to deal with, and she should be doing something about them. Exactly what he wasn't certain, but with Clint gone, she should be around. That much he had confidence in. Lauren would know how to soothe the feathers of some very ruffled clients. Wasn't that what PR gurus did?

Not that he wasn't capable of handling the situations alone, which was exactly what he'd do. "Sylvia, start making arrangements for immediate tech-support travel to Dynamics in Buffalo."

Sylvia snapped to attention. "Jeff and Cecil?" she asked.

Justin nodded. "As always, and anyone else they feel they might need. Dynamics's problem has to be solved on-site. Their whole system went down. Every minute is money. We've got to get them back up and make them impervious to another attack."

The phone was already to Sylvia's ear, and her fingers on the number pad. "Consider it done."

Justin sighed as he went back to his desk. At least he had Sylvia. She called him a few minutes later to tell him flight times and that she'd reached Jeff.

"Hey." Jeff entered Justin's office about five minutes after that. "I just got the page that I'm needed."

"You're needed, all right," Justin said. And despite their differences, it always amazed him just how similar they did look, even at age thirty. Each stood six foot one, each had light reddish blond hair and cream-colored skin. Not one freckle remained from either of their childhoods.

"So what's going on?" Jeff asked. "I heard we've got major problems."

"We do. Dynamics got hit with a virus. We're working on their server issues, but about two dozen of their computers require complete reinstalls. Every minute they're down is costing them millions."

Jeff grinned. There was nothing he loved more than jumping into the fray. He'd wanted to be a firefighter, but asthma had ended that dream, much to his safety-conscious mother's relief. "So when do Cecil and I leave?"

Justin's shoulders slumped as some stress lifted. The best man for any computer-related crisis, Jeff had never let his brothers down. He was their Mr. Fix-it. "The next flight to Buffalo is at eleven. Sylvia's made arrangements to have you both on it. Do you need anyone else?"

"No," Jeff said. He glanced at his Rolex, the watch he'd bought more for its working precision than for its status. "So, like, I'm out of here right now."

Justin nodded. "Exactly."

"Cool. Never a dull moment at this place. Super Jeff off to save the day. This company couldn't survive without me."

For the first time that morning, Justin grinned. "Nope."

"I'll have Lauren feed my cat."

Lauren, who should be in the office. Justin's smile faded and he briefly wondered why she annoyed him so much. She really was a contradiction. Friday, Miss Plain and Mousy had worn a fitted red sweater that had made his libido boil and want to know exactly what lay underneath. As to why she'd crawled under his skin, Justin had no answer. "She's out of the office today."

"Yeah." Jeff shrugged. "I saw her Saturday when I picked up my pinstripe and had her iron my dress pants."

For some reason the thought of Lauren doing Jeff's laundry didn't sit well with Justin. "She irons your clothes?"

Jeff grinned, the grin of a man who has domestic bliss without the emotional entanglements of ring-around-the-finger. "I'm a lucky guy. Anyway, she told me she'd e-mailed you, but she wouldn't tell me why she took today off. Said it was a surprise and I'd have to wait. I guess now I'll have to find out what it is when I get back."

The phone rang and Justin picked it up and listened. "Oh. Okay, Sylvia. No, of course I don't have time for it, but I do want my floors done. My house is a FEMA wanna-be. You know, Federal Emergency Management Association. They go in after disasters. Send the call through." Justin held up a finger, indicating that Jeff should wait. "Justin Wright. Hey, Bob. What's up?"

His contractor's voice boomed through the line and Justin moved the phone farther away from his ear. "Justin, today's the day. We're putting the first coat of polyurethane on your floors. See, I told you we'd be finished way before Christmas."

Finally. They'd been sanding and refinishing the hardwood for almost a week. Besides having furniture in every corner, spare or not, Justin had a fine layer of dust coating everything, even the rooms that had been taped off. "That's great."

Bob chuckled. "I'm glad you think so, because you'll need to be out of your house for about three days while we get everything done."

"What?" That started today? Surely he had heard wrong. "Three days?"

"At least three days. Sorry to spring it on you like this, but of course you want the job done. Remember, I told you about this aspect of the job before we started the project."

Justin sighed. Bob was one of the best floor finishers in St. Louis and he had warned him that the floors couldn't be walked on; even worse there would be the smell to deal with during the sealing process.

"Yeah, I remember. It's okay, Bob. I'll find somewhere to go. Start the work." Justin set down the phone. Mondays sucked. What else could go wrong?

"More problems?" Jeff asked.

Justin craned his neck to relieve some of his growing tension. "Not Wright Solutions–related, at least. They're finally getting around to finishing my hardwood floors. I have to stay out for three days since I won't have a bed and the odor will be terrible. But don't worry about me. You need to get out of here. Time is money and Dynamics is one of our best customers."

"Well, luckily for you, this Dynamics crisis might just be perfect timing. You can stay at my place. I'll leave a spare key underneath my welcome mat." Jeff strode to the door. He grinned as he glanced back over his shoulder. "Just be sure you feed my cat."

PRETTY WOMAN. The words from the Roy Orbison song resonated in Lauren's head long after the tune had faded from St. Louis's classic-oldies radio station. But the words fit. The woman reflected back at her in the rearview mirror *was* pretty. The spa had been worth every penny.

Lauren grinned as she pulled up to an intersection and the guy in the car to her right gave her a second, then a third look. For once Lauren knew it wasn't because she'd had food on her face or something embarrassing like that. For once it was because she really did look good.

She'd entrusted her body to the care of Meredith and

Jacques, and neither of the spa professionals had let her leave disappointed. She'd been made over from head right down to her now bright red toenails.

When they'd finally spun her around after the finishing touches, at first Lauren hadn't believed that she really was the person in the mirror. Jacques had lightened her dark brown hair to a honey hue. He hadn't made her medium blond—he said that would wash her out too much and make her appear trite—but he had lightened every strand and used foils to weave subtle golden strands throughout.

Her eyebrows had been tweezed and shaped, and after applying a natural foundation, Meredith had applied soft blush makeup to Lauren's cheekbones and subtle color to her eyelids. The result? The man in a pickup truck to her left said it best when he gave her a large grin and a thumbs-up before he pulled away.

Lauren smiled and avoided drumming her newly manicured fingernails on the steering wheel, as was her habit. She pulled into Chesterfield Mall and found a spot near an entrance. One stop left to go before her plan was complete. All she needed now was lingerie. The basic cotton underwear she usually wore was not acceptable for tonight's seduction. She wanted lace, the silkier and skimpier the better.

She parked the car, entered the mall and strode into the shop with complete confidence. She knew her body was ready for it—she'd been waxed, buffed and moisturized until every part of her five-foot-six-inch figure glowed. She'd never been fat, and now viewing in the three-way mirror the black lace ensemble she'd found, she felt like one of those credit-card commercials. No matter the cost—the result was worth it. Lauren picked up a pair of thigh-high seamed hose, paid for her purchases and carried the pink-and-white bag with pride.

The December night was brisk, but Lauren didn't feel the cold as she unlocked her Toyota Celica and tossed the bag onto the back seat. Darkness had long ago descended, and Lauren's headlights cut a swath through the starry night as she drove home to her condo. She'd eat a little something just to make sure her stomach didn't growl foolishly, drink a little wine to give her some liquid courage, then she'd dress and walk the twelve feet to Jeff's condo. *Monday Night Football* started at eight. And as much as she loved football, too, tonight was about seduction. Jeff would only get to see about five minutes of the game before her arrival.

Lauren turned up the volume on the radio as a Macy Gray song came on. Singing along, Lauren belted out the words. Even the song was a sign. Today she'd had one good omen after another. *Jeff Wright, here I come. You aren't going to know what hit you.* Every light magically seemed to be green and Lauren grinned. For once, finally, everything was going to be perfect.

JUSTIN WASN'T A CAT PERSON, but that didn't stop Jeff's indoor, with an alley-cat personality, feline from taking permanent residence right on top of Justin's chest.

The monster even purred so loud that Justin couldn't hear the television. If he turned his head to the right he could see the flat screen, though, and thus at least tell what was going on. Reaching for the remote control, a few inches beyond his grasp on the coffee table, meant risking upending the cat with the killer claws. Justin decided that hearing the game, which started in about fifteen minutes, didn't matter.

Like most Saint Louisans he loved the Saint Louis Rams, but tonight he wasn't interested in watching them play the New Orleans Saints. Suddenly extremely exhausted, all Justin wanted right now was sleep.

He'd left the office only about a half hour ago. Jeff had arrived safely in Buffalo and he and Cecil had started pulling the all-nighter required to rebuild Dynamics's systems. Clint had returned from Springfield, soothed the other client's fears, and at last, after sending about a dozen e-mails and signing a dozen letters, Justin had been free to go home. Dinner had been a drive-through-restaurant chicken sandwich that hadn't tasted all that great.

He'd hoped to pick up some essentials at home before going to Jeff's, but upon arriving at his Chesterfield ranch, he'd learned from the note on his front door that he couldn't even enter the house until ten the next morning. He'd said a few words his mother would scold him for before he'd headed to Jeff's.

Thank goodness he and his brother were twins. He'd at least be able to borrow something clean to wear to the office tomorrow. Tonight, though, he wanted to be really comfortable. So, with no change of clothes, Justin had cranked up the heat, stripped to his boxers, grabbed a beer and now found himself used as a cat pillow.

He glanced at the VCR clock. His mother had always said that her twins were opposites, which in many ways they were. Jeff, the computer god and techno wizard, always had his VCR programmed to the proper time, for example. Justin's VCR usually just blinked 12:00 because he was too lazy to set it and he hadn't seen the need to replace the aged unit with one that automatically set the time itself. Now Jeff's VCR said 7:50. Justin had ten minutes before football. Enough for a power nap. After all, his eyelids did feel so heavy. He let his lashes drift down, and soon man and beast fell into easy slumber.

LAUREN LOWERED HER WINEGLASS and looked at the clock on her microwave for the hundredth time. If a watched pot never boiled, then a watched microwave clock never changed. Lauren held her breath as the display finally flickered from 7:59 and became 8:00.

It was finally time.

She took one last reassuring sip of wine. However, the room-temperature Merlot did little to calm her racing heart. She glanced at the bottle. She'd only had two glasses, enough to make her feel warm, fuzzy, brave and wanton. She smoothed out an imaginary wrinkle in her hose. Her outfit was perfect: a merry widow covered by a sheer black robe. Underneath, lacy black garter straps held up the seamed black thigh-highs. Slinky black heels that she'd worn only once graced her feet, her red toenail polish playing peekaboo beneath the sheer hose.

She'd gotten her portable CD player ready. While Jeff had a fantastic stereo complete with surround sound, it would be quicker and easier for her to just use her battery-operated unit and have it on as she entered his condo.

Butterflies flitted in her stomach. She couldn't believe how nervous she was. She'd had relationships before—even lived with a man for three months before he'd cheated on her. But this time was different. This was Jeff, her best friend. Tonight would forever change their relationship. They would go from friends to lovers. He'd realize the pal could also be the girlfriend. They would have it all. She knew he adored her; but still, taking the next step was always risky. She had nothing to fear. Right? She was now a knockout.

The clock finally flickered to 8:05 and Lauren grabbed the CD player. Her ankles wobbled for a brief moment as she rose to her feet.

She put her hand on her condo door and completed the quick run from her door to his. Her key made brief work of the lock and she stepped inside. The room was dark except for the light coming from the television set, and relief filled Lauren. She'd worried for nothing about him seeing her in the bright light. Not only did the low glow cast shadows everywhere, but he was sleeping. Buddy, Jeff's cat, lifted a sleepy head. Lauren put a finger to her lips, suddenly realizing how silly that was—why was she trying to tell a cat to keep quiet? She stifled a nervous giggle and turned on her CD player. It was now or never. In a few moments she would know Jeff Wright more intimately than she'd ever known him. As the slow groove came on, Lauren began to dance.

HE WAS HAVING the most wonderful dream. The noises of the football game that he really couldn't hear anyway had faded, replaced by a deep bluesy voice that he recognized but in his sleep couldn't quite place. Something sweet had reached his seeking nostrils. Roses? Jasmine? Musk? Whatever perfume had permeated his brain brought his body to slow attention.

The cat was gone. Instead, something silky skimmed his chest. Black and white contrasted in the darkness. Oh, my. A garter-covered a thigh.

He hadn't had a dream like this in a long, long while. He shifted, letting the seductive moment of the dream envelop him. A beautiful woman danced for him. Not a professional, either—he'd seen those a few times at bachelor parties—but an amateur. Meaning, much better motivations. Much better movements when they weren't rehearsed. Much more…intriguing. Oh.

As she gyrated her hips and lowered herself toward the floor in a movement bordering on erotic, he groaned. Oh, yes. Whoever his fantasy woman was, she was dancing just for him. And whoever she was, it was his dream, and he would have her or die trying.

He snaked out a hand, his fingers grazing the naked part of her upper thigh. Heat traveled through him and gathered lower. Her bottom lip dropped into a playful pout and she waved her forefinger at him in a no-no movement as she stepped away from his outstretched hand. Did she say, "Not until the song's over"?

Who cared about the song? As her lips neared his, *he* sure didn't. Excitement overtook him and he leaned up to catch her lips, but she'd drawn away. Kiss me! He wanted to see her face. Instead, he saw black lace covering creamy white breasts. Oh. He swallowed as part of him roused to painful attention. Sanity fled. He'd been a year without a woman, so no wonder the intensity filling him. She glanced back again, her black robe skimming his bare chest. His lips opened and his head arched. Did his mystery woman know what she did to him?

Of course she did. The song playing in his head crescendoed and as it began to wind down she moved closer. He willed the dream to brighten, but, backlit by the television, the dream refused. Suddenly, her body sat next to his. "Hey," she said.

Did he answer her? He wasn't sure what he said, for when her lips touched the side of his jaw, he lost all control. He reached forward, fisted his hands into that long hair that had been calling him and brought her lips down to his.

The rockets he'd made as a kid didn't have anything on the explosion now shooting through him as he kissed her. He ravaged her mouth, tasting his dream woman's sweet kiss. Never had he had a dream so real or so good, and he refused to question it lest it dissipate before he'd fully enjoyed it. His hand cupped her breast, the black lace texture tempting his fingers to slide beneath. She gasped against his mouth as he pearled a nipple, and she fell closer to him.

He didn't want to let her mouth go, but he wanted to taste her, to lick the creamy valley between and taste those hardened peaks themselves.

All he had to do was roll her over. He encircled her waist and turned her so that her back pressed against the couch. Her stocking-covered legs wound around his bare ones. Damn, he wanted her. His body throbbed and he thrust his tongue back into her mouth. As she returned his kiss, her throaty moan tormented him further.

He pulled away a little, his fingers pushing the merry widow down. She was beautiful and he longed to see her face. He forced his eyes to adjust to the dim light and then he forced himself to picture her face. And then he could see her. Her eyes were closed, but something was so familiar. Lauren? He was dreaming of Lauren.

No. This couldn't be Lauren. Lauren didn't wear smoky makeup or have hair the color of honey. He'd dreamed of Lauren once, more than a year ago, but she'd never looked like this. She certainly hadn't been a siren. She'd never made his body respond, never turned him into a randy teenage schoolboy.

She leaned to kiss him again and he let those provocative lips send him spinning. His body ached with need and Justin clung to the dream.

"Oh, Jeff."

Every inch of Justin stilled as if cold water had just drenched him. Sharp painful awareness filled him. This wasn't a dream.

And if this wasn't a dream…

He was really kissing Lauren. Denial sounded in his brain. No. Jeff and Lauren weren't… Jeff would have said something. Warned him. Jeff always confided in Justin. Always.

Reality slapped Justin upside the head. He'd been kissing Lauren. She'd been trying to seduce Jeff. She thought he was Jeff. She didn't realize… "Lauren!"

Her eyes flew open. "Jeff?"

Somehow Justin stood, and already Lauren was scrambling off the couch and to her feet. "This was a bad idea. I'm sorry, I…"

Where was that light? Justin fumbled for the switch, wishing for once that those clap-on, clap-off devices weren't so silly and that people like his brother actually bought them. His fingers found the knob and he flipped it. Harsh white light flooded the room.

He saw the exact moment that her realization of his identity dawned. Her well-kissed and swollen lips opened in shocked disbelief. Horror claimed those deep brown eyes. He knew exactly what she saw—his near nakedness and his now-softening arousal. Her hand flew to her lips, she gathered her arms around her lace-covered chest, and before Justin could even think of stopping her, she slammed out the front door.

Chapter Three

She'd been kissing Justin! Lauren leaned against her front door for a brief moment to gather her wits. Lock. She needed to lock the door. To her dismay, her hand shook so much that it took her two tries to place the security chain in its holder. The dead bolt, at least, turned easily under her fumbling fingers.

But the fact that her door was now locked didn't ease her fears. Dear Lord. How had this happened? She'd been kissing the wrong Wright!

Her chest heaved and she could hear the voice of her yoga instructor. Take deep calming breaths. Deep calming breaths. Lauren tried, but those miraculous deep calming breaths her instructor swore by didn't help. No, right now Lauren still wanted to drop through the floor and bury herself six feet under, forever and ever. She'd been kissing Justin Wright!

She hated Justin. Thought he was the scourge of the planet. He annoyed her. He was rude. A jerk. A womanizer. See? She had proof. He'd ravaged her and… It had been good. Oh, so very good. His kisses had sent shivers to her curling toes.

No! She tried to wipe the kiss away, but her lips still tingled from the touch of his. Think of Jeff. She wanted Jeff, sweet adorable Jeff. Not his wicked playboy twin who was a constant thorn in her side.

Hot tears filled Lauren's eyes and she mentally berated herself. How could this have happened? What was Justin doing at Jeff's? And despite the fact that he shouldn't have been there in the first place, how could she have made such a terrible mistake? Sure, the room had been dark except for the TV. But she should have known. She should have been able to tell the difference between the two brothers. They wore their watches on different wrists. Shouldn't that have been an early clue that she had the wrong man? But she'd been so swept away!

So, instead of Jeff, she'd kept right on kissing Justin! Now her tears fell freely, ruining the makeup that Meredith had spent two painstaking hours perfecting. Lauren buried her face in her hands for a long anguished moment. Then, in an attempt to cleanse herself of the memory of Justin's tantalizing touch, Lauren entered the bedroom and stripped off the offending clothes. She tossed the whole lingerie outfit into the deep recesses of her walk-in closet. She preferred never to see it again. The outfit had worked, all right, but not on the right brother.

How did one recover from this gaffe? Did one? Thank God, Justin had said something or she'd have been the making of a Jerry Springer show. Lauren pulled on her warm flannel pajamas, the gown dropping reassuringly to her feet and covering every inch of her body. Jeff had given her the Lang gown last Christmas, and whereas the merry widow had revealed everything, the flannel gown showed absolutely nothing from her neck down.

Lauren didn't want to face her reflection in the mirror, but she had to. Haunted brown eyes stared back at her. Despite the smearing of her mascara, she still saw traces of Meredith's miraculous work. All for naught.

Lauren banged her fist on the marble countertop and grabbed a washcloth. Within minutes, she'd washed away the pretty woman men had glanced at more than once. In her place returned ordinary Lauren, who still appeared shell-shocked from discovering she'd been kissing Justin Wright.

Worse, she'd discovered that kissing him had been nothing short of phenomenal. Never before had a kiss sent *those* sensations to her toes. Never before had fingertips on her breasts sent such heat pooling through her. Wine. She nodded false hope to her reflection. It had been wine and adrenaline. That was all. Nothing else. She'd just gotten caught up in the seductive dance, caught up in the magical moment. For once, she'd been a woman in control, in charge of the seduction she'd initiated. That was what had made even the kisses seem larger than life, better than any other man she'd ever kissed.

It had nothing to do with the fact that the person she'd been kissing had been Justin Wright.

Nothing at all.

Lauren squared her chin and stared at herself in the mirror, but that brought fresh tears to her eyes as her former bravado failed her. She'd kissed Justin.

How did one go from kissing one brother to the other? Should she say to Jeff, "Oops, I made a mistake. Forgive me?" Beg Justin not to say a word? She didn't want to see Justin at work now, much less talk about what she'd been trying to do.

She wasn't the type to keep secrets, especially from her best friend, but for this once she'd have to try. She couldn't tell Jeff. Such a perfect seduction—wasted on the wrong man. So much for good omens. She'd lost before she'd really begun.

The doorbell to her condo began shrilling. "Go away," Lauren called, but she knew that whoever was at the door couldn't hear her. She pulled on her cowprint slippers and plodded her way to the front door. As she put her eye to the peephole, her fear was confirmed. Justin stood on the other side.

"Go away," she yelled again.

"No," he replied. "Let me in. We need to talk."

He was the last person she wanted to talk to. Hadn't she just thought that she'd prefer never to even see him again?

"No, we don't need to talk," Lauren said. "I've got nothing to say to you. It was all a big mistake. A misunderstanding. Ha-ha. Okay, we've shared a laugh. Now go away!"

"No. Be reasonable and let me in. If you don't, I've got Jeff's key."

She pressed her eye to the peephole again and jumped back as she realized he was attempting to stare in. She backed away. Her voice quivered slightly as she said, "The key's useless. The chain's on."

His powerful voice boomed through the closed door. "I'll break your damn door down if I have to, Lauren. It won't take me but a good kick, and believe me, I can afford the damage."

Her heart raced. He wouldn't really kick her door down, right? Although, with her short tenure at Wright Solutions and her three years as Jeff's neighbor, she knew that when Justin said something, he meant business. But kicking her door down? Of course not. Still, she said, "I'll have you arrested for breaking and entering."

"And I'll tell Jeff exactly what happened between us, exactly what you were attempting to do."

A silence fell, and Lauren slumped against the doorway. Damn him, but on that count, he had her. Jeff knowing, and hearing, about her indiscretion from his twin brother was the last thing she wanted or needed.

"It's cold out here, Lauren. All I'm wearing is a

sweatshirt and jeans. Do I need to count? I'll give you until three. One…two…"

Lauren opened the door.

Justin stepped into the condo, a burst of cold winter air arriving with him. His green-eyed gaze flicked over her as he appraised her quickly. "I liked the other outfit better."

Heat filled her cheeks and she knew her face reddened. She leaned against the front door for much-needed support. "It wasn't for you."

He raked a hand through his hair. "Duh. As if I didn't figure that out. I thought I was dreaming. Hell of a dream, though."

Justin cocked his head and surveyed her. Lauren's toes tingled in her slippers and she scrunched them to end the annoying sensation. "Although I admit it's too bad. Your outfit was a lot better than that granny gown. A hell of a lot better. I liked it a lot. Oh, yeah, a lot."

Justin attempted a grin, but the moment he did, he acknowledged it was hopeless. He couldn't melt her icy reserve or bring down the walls she'd built in just a few minutes. Already he could see that she'd stripped off the makeup. She couldn't change her hair color, though, that soft honey shade that shimmered and called to a man. He liked it. Aw, hell.

Couldn't she tell that this was an awkward situation for him, too? It wasn't often that a man thought he was dreaming, woke up to discover that the beautiful woman was real and then learned that the sweet kisses she was bestowing were actually meant for someone else. Lauren had left him in quite a painful state, and as he'd pulled on a pair of Jeff's jeans and a sweatshirt, Justin had decided that reality, like Mondays, also sucked.

She was his employee, and he'd practically given her a tonsillectomy with his tongue. He'd had his hands on her breasts. Her nipples had pebbled between his fingers. He'd even…

He shoved all those tormenting thoughts aside. All they were doing was getting him aroused again. At the very least he had to work with Lauren. And if she got her way, got what she wanted from the seduction, she might even become his future sister-in-law. That thought wasn't pleasant, but for her sake and his, he was determined to make the best of the awkward situation.

"I came to apologize," he said. She gazed at him skeptically. A movement caught his eye and he glanced down. Her foot was wiggling inside the slipper as if she was attempting to tap her foot. Were those actually cow faces on her feet? He yanked his gaze upward, and this time it landed on the small pink bow located at the center of the ruffle. Right where her breasts met.

Despite the concealing flannel fabric, Justin's mind went into overdrive picturing what lay beneath. He raised his eyes, now getting a good view of her new hairdo. Wow. Even now his fingers itched to again touch the honey-colored strands.

"You were saying?" Lauren prompted.

He tried to focus, but what he really wanted to do was pick her up, carry her to bed and strip off the offending flannel that tormented him. "Justin?"

"Oh, yeah. God, Lauren, this sounds so lame. And I am sorry. I thought I was dreaming. I didn't realize I wasn't until, well…" He paused because she appeared stricken again. "I realized I wasn't dreaming when you called me Jeff. I'm assuming you thought I was him."

Lauren was suddenly in motion, her slippers shuffling as she strode past him. Worried she was going to flee, Justin put out his hand and grabbed her arm. Despite the gown's long sleeve, electricity flared through him, sending a spark all the way to his feet.

"Static," he said. The wide-eyed look on her face told him she'd felt it, too, and that she knew he'd lied about the cause. But she'd stopped her flight, and he dropped his arm to his side. He shoved his hand into his front jeans pocket.

"We need to talk about what happened," Justin reiterated.

Lauren shook her head so furiously that locks of her hair fell into her face. His fingers desired to push the wayward strands away.

"No," she said. "We don't need to talk. We pretend it didn't happen. We don't tell Jeff. We ignore each other at work. That's all we need to do and everything will be fine."

He wished it were just that simple. "Lauren, I kissed you."

Her chin jutted forward into that stubborn line he'd seen so many times at the office. "So what if you kissed me? I'm sure you kiss a lot of women. And it was just a kiss." Her face reddened. "And okay, maybe a little more. But it meant nothing. I'd had a few glasses of wine. Plus, I didn't know it was you."

Ouch. True, perhaps, but actually hearing the words certainly dented his male ego and pride. He'd kissed her, and it had been fantastic. Better than fantastic. Perhaps he shouldn't have been celibate for a year.

He focused on Lauren's lips. Even devoid of all gloss and color, they were beautiful. As was she. Had he never really seen her before this moment? He sobered slightly. Jeff probably hadn't, either, which was why she'd chosen to seduce him. Stupid lucky guy.

"Listen, Justin, if we both purge the memory from our brains, then we can simply rewrite history and pretend tonight didn't happen. Okay? Besides, isn't that what men do all the time?"

No, it wasn't, and her perfect PR answer was not okay. He frowned. Was it really that easy for women to write something off? The memory of her kiss and the feel of her body would be etched in his brain for quite a while to come. But, Justin's mama had raised her boys to be chivalrous. This situation certainly called for that. "All right. If that's the way you want it and if you can live with that decision, well, so can I. We'll purge our memories. Pretend tonight didn't happen."

"Good." Lauren nodded and her hair fell about her shoulders. He stifled a groan. Sleep would not be at all peaceful tonight.

"Anyway, now that we've got this situation settled…" Her voice trailed off and she glanced at the door.

A sense of letdown filled him and Lauren's dismissal didn't sit well. "You want me to go."

"If I'm not being too rude," Lauren said. "I think I want to get some sleep. I have a busy day tomorrow, what with being off today. I'm sure there were things that I missed."

She'd missed all the company crises, but Justin didn't care about those anymore. This crisis was more important. He stared at her, seeing her flushed face, the subtle impatience in her features. She'd covered her embarrassment admirably, and thus his respect for her grew. No, now wasn't the time to fill her in on all the crises that the company had handled today.

"Yeah, you probably do have a busy day," Justin said. He felt more awkward than a kid on his first date. His brother was way too fortunate and Justin had the urge to beat Jeff up the moment he returned from Buffalo, just for old times' sake. "I guess I'll see you at the office."

"Sure," Lauren said with a relieved nod. "It'll be fine, really. Nothing will change and everything will be just as it was before. You'll see."

Somehow Justin didn't believe her as he went back over to his brother's condo. No, he'd kissed her. All she'd done was make him see her differently: see her as a desirable woman, instead of just an employee with lots of expensive ideas. No, he doubted anything could be the same between them again.

JUSTIN WRIGHT TOSSED the briefcase down. It landed on his desk with an annoying thump. Tuesdays should be outlawed, especially Tuesdays following long, sleepless Monday nights filled with erotic and sexy dreams of Lauren Brown. "Sylvia!"

Sylvia entered his office and arched an eyebrow at him. "Yes?"

"Is Lauren in?"

"Of course she is. Her personal day was yesterday, remember?"

Justin attempted to put out of his mind the erotic image of just how personal that day had gotten. "So she's here."

"I said she was. You're the one who's fashionably late," Sylvia pointed out.

Justin grimaced. "I didn't sleep well last night, so when I finally did I caught a few extra Zs. I'm staying at Jeff's until my floors are done." He suddenly made a fist. "Why am I explaining myself? You're my secretary, not my mother."

Sylvia's eyes twinkled and she shrugged. "Who

knows? Anyhow, would you like me to fetch Lauren for you?"

Justin shook his head. "No, I'll go find her. Later. Right now I need the Peters report and my mail."

"I'll get both." Sylvia left the office. She stuck her head back in. "Do you want some coffee? You seem like you could use caffeine. I just made a fresh pot."

"Sure," Justin growled. For the next few minutes he buried himself in his work, then finally pushed the meeting minutes aside. He had to admit: his concentration was shot. His eyelids felt heavy, and for a moment he let them drift mercifully closed. Maybe here in the office he wouldn't picture Lauren dancing half-naked, feel the touch of her lips on his.

"Sleeping on the job?"

His eyes flew open. He recognized *that* voice. "Lauren."

"I ran into Sylvia in the kitchen. She said you were asking about me."

Lauren held out a steaming mug of coffee, and their fingers touched briefly as he took the mug from her. Just like last night, Justin felt electricity spark between them. He resolved to turn up the humidifiers.

"So when you asked Sylvia if I was here, did you need something, or were you afraid I would take a sick day, that I somehow couldn't face you?"

No, that wasn't it at all, but now that she was in his office, he wasn't ready to face her.

At least not yet.

He had to get himself together. She'd tormented his dreams, and now here she was in the flesh. Bad verbiage. Here she was, standing in front of him.

Oh, whatever. He tossed aside his attempts at proper semantics. For even though she wore a plain boring business skirt and nondescript beige blouse instead of that tight red sweater like Friday, Justin could no longer envision plain old Lauren Brown. Her hair color was different, her makeup had changed. But the real reason was that *he* had changed. His body had felt hers, and it was a fresh, delectable memory despite its ending. Try as he might, Justin didn't see his PR employee; instead, he still saw the siren who'd danced, who'd called to him and seduced him with a spiraling kiss.

"So, did you have something you needed?" Lauren asked again.

Yeah, he needed, all right. He needed to get Lauren out of his system. Unfortunately, tossing her over his desk was sexual harassment, and the other option— sending her far away to Siberia—also wouldn't work. She had a job to do, and she wanted his brother.

Heck, no one had ever really wanted nerdy Jeff over supercool Justin, at least in the long-term, forever way. But Lauren did.

Worse, he couldn't take on the challenge. He couldn't pursue her, topple her defenses, capture those lips again in a mind-numbing kiss. She didn't want him, and while he could get her to desire him physically and get her to beg for his touch, he'd grown tired of those juvenile games aeons ago. As it was, she didn't respect him. And respect was what he craved. His mother had raised a chivalrous man, despite what some might think.

He tried to cover. "Actually, I'm glad you're here. I wanted to talk to you, to make sure we're still squared away about last night."

Lauren's eyes darted around Justin's office as if she was afraid someone else might be listening. "What was last night?"

One spectacular moment that had been blasted away. Justin inhaled a deep breath. "Let me use another tactic. Since we all work together, I wanted to make peace *and* offer to help you."

Did her eyebrow have to look that sexy when it arched? Sylvia's never did, which was why after five years she was still his secretary. That and she was his mother's age. "Help me?" Lauren asked.

Justin struggled for some semblance of control. He hadn't meant to wing this. "Well, yeah. The way I figure it is this: You want Jeff. You like Jeff. I know my brother. He's like mud. Dense and clueless. He probably has no idea you like him or want him. Thus, last night's very sexy seduction attempt."

Hoping to eliminate her deer-in-the-headlights expression, Justin pressed on. He'd always been cool with the ladies, a master of the words. Now he was making a bad situation worse. "What I mean to say is that I feel horrible that I messed everything up. I want to make it up to you. The only way I can figure out how to put things right is to help you win over the man of your dreams."

Her look was disbelieving and dubious. "Man of my dreams?"

"Jeff. My brother. He is, isn't he? The man of your dreams?"

A regretful twinge filled Justin as for a moment her face appeared dreamy. Then her skeptical facade returned. "And if he is?"

"The way I figure it is this. You need some help in getting him to notice you. Not that last night, ah, probably wouldn't work again." *It sure worked for me,* Justin didn't add. "Anyway, I can give you that help. I know my brother better than anyone. Perhaps it's that twin thing. You'd be good for him. Probably too good, even."

As Lauren's skepticism changed into a small tentative smile, Justin felt a glimmer of hope. "Thank you. You *are* surprising."

Now it was his turn to be confused. "I am?"

"Yes. You're not half as bad as I thought. You've handled this situation rather well, and I appreciate that you think I'm too good for him."

"Uh, gee," Justin said, kicking himself for how lame that sounded. Here he was, as gawky as a teenager instead of the suave businessman he'd become.

Lauren smiled suddenly, and Justin's gut clenched. He gulped some coffee, the hot liquid burning his tongue because he drank it too fast. His only reward was that she hadn't noticed his painful wince.

"You know, perhaps you're not all of what your playboy reputation or your brutish office mannerisms make you out to be. It's sweet of you to offer. Really, no offense meant, but I'll handle this situation my way."

Playboy rep? Brutish office mannerisms? Okay, he could live with that. He was a bit forceful. However, he was not a playboy, and hearing the word, especially from Lauren's lips, stung. His going without sex for a year had been a conscious choice—that of a man who didn't need to keep his bed warm just so he could rut. "Okay, then. I just thought I could give you some tips, help you somehow. To compensate for last night."

"I understand, and it's a generous gesture. But I'll deal with Jeff in my own time. What I'd like from you is just your sworn secrecy."

"My lips are sealed," Justin said. He enjoyed some morbid satisfaction that Lauren's brown eyes darkened. After all, as he took another sip of the burning, biting black coffee, chivalry sucked.

"You look great, Lauren. I like your hair. You'll have to tell me later where you went."

"Thanks, Sylvia," Lauren said as she passed Justin's secretary's desk. "I promise to tell you. But remind me."

"I'll hold you to that. I'm sure you're a bit behind after yesterday."

"That I am," Lauren said, rounding the corner and putting space between her body and Justin's office. Moments after he'd cracked that "lips are sealed" comment, she'd voiced her excuses and fled.

She didn't ever want to remember or think about Justin's lips in any context. She'd been trying to erase the memory of those spectacular kisses ever since they'd happened.

As for accepting his help, the farther away from him she stayed, the better. Justin Wright raised dangerous sensations in her. She couldn't trust dangerous sensations. They'd gotten her in trouble once before, with Mike. She'd thought he'd changed his playboy ways, until three months after moving in with him she'd discovered another woman's panties in her bed. Thankfully, she hadn't joined bank accounts the way Mike had been pressing her to do.

Justin had some of the same playboy manner. She'd seen him run through women, although she had to admit she hadn't seen him run through any lately. But then, he wasn't at Jeff's as often as he had been in the past.

Too bad he'd chosen last night to be there. And he had kissed her. Dream or no dream, that wasn't an excuse. That was why she liked Jeff. Jeff, who was nice, safe and secure, not a playboy like his brother. That was what she envisioned for her future. Wasn't it?

For a moment, her head clouded and she wasn't sure. She shook her head and cleared her thoughts. Outside her window a man was parking his nice family sedan and entering the neighboring building. That was what Jeff was. A family sedan. Dependable. Reliable. They just needed to add some speed to their relationship. She didn't desire another Mike and all his idle promises.

She pressed a finger to her lips. Justin Wright, despite his tantalizing touch, was wrong for her. All wrong.

And she had too much work to do to worry about him anymore. Giving herself a nod of encouragement, she pushed his memory away.

Chapter Four

"So, did you miss me?" Jeff's infectious grin widened, and despite her earlier misgivings about what would happen upon seeing him again, Lauren smiled right back.

She pointed to the huge basket of laundry he carried in his arms. "I don't think I missed you that much."

Jeff's grin turned sheepish. "Nah, probably not, but to make up for it, I'll buy the Chinese food that's on its way."

"Ooh, sold," Lauren said. She opened her front door wider, the cold air coming to swirl around her bare feet. In a moment she'd put her cow slippers on. "I guess you can come in."

"Thanks." Jeff bumped Lauren's Christmas wreath as he entered the condo and made his way to her laundry closet. She straightened the wreath out and closed the door. "You know, one of these days I will buy a washer and dryer," he called back over his shoulder.

"You keep promising," Lauren said as she followed him into her kitchen.

Jeff set the laundry basket on the kitchen table. "No, not promising, just saying. There's a difference."

"Yeah, which is why you're always here with your laundry basket."

He pulled open the double doors that concealed the washer and dryer. "Oh, come on. It's your wonderful company."

"I just live closer than your mother," Lauren said. "And she'd harp on you about finding a wife."

"True," Jeff acknowledged. "You're cuter than my mom, too." He opened the washing-machine lid, turned around and squinted for a moment. "Did you do something with your hair?"

"I had it cut and colored."

"Looks good," Jeff said as he dumped the basket out onto the table. "So was that the surprise?"

As if he'd really noticed, Lauren thought. He'd hardly glanced at her hair. But then, why should he? She was only a pal. She sighed, but as he sorted his whites from his darks, Jeff didn't notice her resignation. "That was the surprise," she said.

"Cool. So, did you catch the game Monday night?" Jeff asked.

"No," Lauren said quickly.

Jeff paused from loading the dark clothes into the washer. His eyes narrowed. "I don't believe it. You missed *Monday Night Football?* What happened? That's unreal."

Lauren thought quickly. "Yeah, I know. But my mom wanted some help putting up her Christmas tree. And since you were out of town…"

"Too bad. You missed a great game. Even listening to the game being streamed live over the Internet was better than nothing." The image of domestic bachelor bliss, Jeff poured liquid soap into the washer. "At least Justin fed my cat. Seen much of him lately?"

"Your cat?"

"Ha-ha. You've become a joker since I left for Buffalo. I meant my brother."

"Just at work," Lauren replied.

"He didn't have any parties, no hot babes all over the place?"

Not unless she'd now be considered a hot babe. And of course he'd stopped before "having" her. "No. It was pretty quiet. I didn't even notice he was there."

Superstition had her crossing her fingers behind her back just to be on the safe side.

Jeff shook his head in disbelief as he turned the washer on. "The boy must be slipping. He hasn't dated anyone serious in quite a while. A year, I think. Rather unlike him. Perhaps I should sign him up for one of those dating services, like that 'just lunch' one. Or force him to place a personal ad or something the way we did Jared. I'll have to mull it over."

"Maybe he's finally maturing."

"Nah, his babe-of-the-month-club subscription probably expired," Jeff said. He pressed Start and the washer began filling. "It is Christmas. Maybe I'll get him another one. Hmm. Think that's a good idea?"

Lauren didn't want to talk about Justin or his legion of past women. She avoided the question by changing the subject. "So, how was your mother's birthday party?"

Jeff tossed the whites back into the laundry basket. "Good. She loved her gifts and hounded us to get married so that we can give her grandbabies. She said cats and computers don't cut it."

"That would be your mom." Lauren had met Mrs. Wright on quite a few occasions when she'd visited Jeff.

"She's definitely got a mind of her own," Jeff said. "She keeps telling us she wants granddaughters. I think she's tired of being surrounded by all boys at family gatherings. Justin and I are hoping that Jared will take the heat off." Jeff paused as a knock sounded on Lauren's front door. "Come on in," he called.

Lauren frowned. "Food already?"

Jeff shook his head. "Too soon. I only phoned them about ten minutes ago, right before I came over here. I wanted to wait until after Justin arrived so he could eat, too. I'd never hear the end of it otherwise."

Justin was coming? Lauren blinked as a stone dropped in her stomach. She'd envisioned a quiet evening with Jeff. She tried to focus on what Jeff was saying. "I left a message on the counter for Justin to head over when he got home. Tonight's hopefully his last night staying at my place. I'm getting sick of him."

Justin's grin was infectious as he entered the small kitchen, but to Lauren his smile spelled doom. "Yeah, I'm getting sick of you, too. Plus, I'm tired of wearing your clothes."

Jeff laughed. "You just don't have any style or taste."

"I do, too," Justin retorted. Lauren knew the brothers were teasing each other.

"You're lucky business casual is now an art form." Jeff rummaged in Lauren's refrigerator and removed a bottle of the beer Lauren kept just for him. Except for an occasional one during *Monday Night Football,* she rarely drank beer. "Want one?" Jeff asked his brother.

"Sure," Justin said. He glanced at Lauren. She glanced at her feet. "Hello, Lauren."

"Hello, Justin," Lauren replied. She picked up the laundry basket and moved it to the floor. Two seconds without having to look at him. She closed the closet doors—three seconds more. So much for her Thursday evening. She'd been avoiding Justin for two days, ever since the encounter in his office. She'd been doing a good job of it up until this point.

Justin brushed by her, his arm accidentally touching hers. Lauren sat down in her kitchen chair with a thump.

Jeff was wrong. It didn't matter what Justin wore. He had style. Loads of it. Even now, dressed in a St. Louis Blues hockey sweatshirt and faded black denim jeans,

Justin created an undeniable presence in the small kitchen.

No! Lauren shook her head fiercely. Somehow she had to get Justin Wright out of her mind; somehow she had to make the situation work. Jeff. She loved Jeff. Right? He was her dream man. The weird feelings she'd been having about Justin these past few days were simply an aberration. Stress. That was all. Stress over the situation. Nothing more.

"Are you okay?" Justin hovered over her and she shifted her body to the opposite side of the chair.

"I'm fine. Just an ear tickle. I hate when that happens." Lauren pulled on her ear and avoided Justin's probing gaze.

"Really?" Justin's arched eyebrow indicated his disbelief, and under his studious appraisal, Lauren began to flush.

"Wow. You get those, too?" Jeff asked. He paused and peeled the label from the longneck bottle and he stuck it on the counter and returned to the kitchen table. He handed Justin a beer. "When I was a kid I used to have tubes in my ears. I hated it. Sometimes I think I can still feel them."

Beer in hand, Justin sat down at the kitchen table next to Lauren. "You always were strange," he said to his brother.

"Yeah, well, look who's talking. We split the same genes."

Justin sipped his beer before saying, "Yeah, well, if so, I got the better half. I'm not the one who can't do my own laundry."

Jeff sat down. Lauren was now flanked by the two men. "I *am* doing my own laundry. I poured in the soap and turned on the machine. See? Listen and you can hear it agitating."

"She ironed your shirt last weekend." Justin swallowed more beer as Jeff shrugged.

"So," Jeff said, letting the words *And your point is?* remain unspoken.

"Lauren may be your neighbor, but she's not your servant or your maid," Justin said.

"Lauren is right here and I can speak for myself. Really, I don't mind. Jeff and I have been doing laundry together for years." She made the mistake of locking gazes with Justin to emphasize her point. Big mistake. Those dark green eyes held something indescribable and her toes started to tingle. She forced her gaze away.

"How homey," Justin said, his sarcasm a tad obvious.

Used to his brother, Jeff remained unperturbed. "Cheaper than buying a machine, and I hate Laundromats."

"Jeff is welcome to do his laundry here whenever he wants. He doesn't need to find a bimbo like you do."

Justin's voice cut a steel edge. "I don't have a bimbo. I have a house with a washer and dryer in the basement. I've done my own laundry since I was in college. My brother is just lazy, and he shouldn't prey on your generosity."

"He's not preying. I offered. It's none of your business, anyway," Lauren snapped. Sitting next to Justin made her feel as agitated as the clothes in the washing machine.

"You're up to your elbows in his boxers every weekend. I'm just saying he should do more than provide Chinese food."

Lauren's jaw jutted forward in the stubborn manner Justin had been subjected to many times the past six months. She was digging in, ready to argue her point until she won or they came to an impasse. Not that this argument was a good idea in the first place. She wanted Jeff to notice her, but probably not the way he was. Right now Jeff was staring at the two of them with obvious avid curiosity, the look on his face one that Justin knew all too well.

While his brother might lack some social graces and prefer a computer to a woman most of the time, Jeff made up for his nerdiness with a razor-sharp intuition. And Jeff wasn't the one who had been having sleepless nights lately.

"Did something happen while I was gone?" Jeff asked. He put his empty beer bottle back on the table.

"No," Lauren and Justin said at the same time. Jeff's eyes narrowed, a sign that problem-solving Jeff had caught a whiff that something wasn't quite right here.

"I'm not so sure," Jeff said.

He and Justin both stared at Lauren. She was studying the closet doors as if they were the most fascinating shade of white she'd ever seen. "It looks like you two got into it," Jeff said.

The words Justin knew were coming soon followed. "So what happened between you? Something did."

"NOTHING." The word from Lauren's mouth came sharp and quick. "Nothing happened," Lauren added. She gave Jeff a smile. "Okay, we quibbled at work a bit over the funding for my marketing strategies. Justin had to apologize, he was so rude."

Jeff glanced from one to the other. "So you two had a fight while I was gone? Argue about the Christmas party again?"

Justin spoke up. "Something like that. She's right when she said I was a little rude in the conference room last week. I had an overseas call and I had to rush out. Clint was there. You can ask him."

"Why do I need to ask him?" Jeff glanced from one to the other. A tension definitely existed in the room. And Lauren did appear different. He glanced back and forth between the two again. Neither of their reassuring smiles quite reached their eyes.

"I'll just take you at your word," Jeff said slowly. He focused on Justin. Having grown up with his twin since the womb, he knew something was wrong.

And he knew it had to do with Lauren. She gazed over Justin's head as if he didn't even exist. Justin was staring at his beer as though it were the first one he'd ever seen. Jeff couldn't help himself. He laughed.

Justin looked up sharply. "What's so funny?"

"Oh, nothing. I was just remembering this joke I heard while fixing Dynamics's computers. Two men were in a bar and—"

"I'll pass," Justin interrupted, just as Jeff had known he would. "Is that food ever going to get here? I brought some work home."

"It should be here soon," Jeff said. He grinned to himself again. Whatever had happened while he was gone was more than a simple fight.

As for his lying brother, Jeff would lay a year's salary that Lauren's makeover had done its job. Justin had a thing for Lauren. He might not even yet realize it himself, but Jeff definitely had noticed the tension between the two over the past six months—

A knock on the door broke the now-endless silence.

"Food," Jeff said. "Hey, Lauren, by the way, I like your Christmas tree. It's festive in here."

"Thanks," she said.

As he went to the front door, Jeff saw a look of something he couldn't quite decipher pass between Justin and Lauren. Yes, Jeff decided as he opened the door and paid the deliveryman, this might be the answer to a growing problem. With Jared out of town, Jeff would need help. Clint certainly needed to hear about this.

"SO WHAT'S GOING ON between you and Lauren?"

Justin turned sharply. After a night finishing laundry, eating sweet-and-sour chicken and enduring Jeff's saccharine smile that said his brother knew something was up, the last thing Justin wanted was to discuss Lauren, especially the very minute he and Jeff returned to Jeff's condo.

Justin himself wasn't sure what was going on. The easy camaraderie, the way she and Jeff had bantered once the Chinese food had arrived, was annoying. Jeff and Lauren had a friendship that Justin had never yet found with any woman.

Until now he'd never had any real jealousy toward his brother. When Lauren had flaunted folding Jeff's boxers, Justin had desired to shred the offending garments. Tonight the green-eyed monster of jealousy had flared, and as much as he wanted to, Justin couldn't discuss why with his brother. He'd promised.

And even if he hadn't, he sure wasn't going to answer Jeff's question about what was going on. *Mortifying* didn't come close to describing finding out that the most phenomenal kisses you'd ever had were meant for someone else.

So instead of answering, Justin evaded the question

by countering with one of his own. "I should ask you the same thing. What's going on with you and Lauren? You seem like an old married couple, the way you swap food and watch TV together. I felt like a third wheel. I was waiting for someone to whip out the baby booties."

Jeff's face paled and he lost his grip on the laundry basket for a moment. He set the basket down on the coffee table and took a moment to regain his composure. "You've got to be kidding, right? Me married? Baby booties? No way. I'm not ready for that old ball and chain."

"You could have fooled me. You and Lauren seem close, and after all, you did get her the job at Wright Solutions."

"Yeah, but our relationship isn't like that. We don't have a relationship. Not like that. Lauren's a great friend. My best gal pal. Probably my best friend besides you and Clint. I can't tell you how many times she's saved my rear end."

"So?" Justin pressed. "I mean, you have no decorations in your apartment except for that small tabletop Christmas tree over there. Let me guess. Lauren bought it for you."

Jeff's guilty look told Justin the truth. Jeff's arms dropped to his side as he shrugged suddenly. "So what? It's just a tree. At least I have one. Your house is totally bare."

"My floors are getting refinished. So tell me, you've known her for what, four years?"

Jeff's forehead creased. "Three. What's that got to do with anything?"

"That's longer than you've been with anyone. So, what do you think about Lauren? Do you like her?"

Jeff's eyes revealed his growing panic as his brother went in for the kill. "Well, yeah. Of course I do. As a friend."

Justin pressed harder. "It couldn't be more? Have you ever asked her? Maybe she likes you. And she is pretty hot, especially with that new hairdo."

Jeff refused to surrender. Instead, he planted his hands on his hips and dug in. "Could you tell me just where you're going with this?"

Where was he going? Justin wasn't quite sure. This chivalry thing of fixing up your brother with a girl you yourself craved was new to Justin. Still, he had to make an attempt, learn by experience, that sort of thing. Give it the old college try. Yeah, that was it.

"I'm just saying that maybe you should look at Lauren. I mean, really look at Lauren. She did her hair differently and she's even prettier now than she was before. Not that she's ever been anywhere near ugly. You could do much worse. And she's obviously fond of laundry and being domestic. She sounds perfect for you."

Jeff crossed his arms and stared at his brother. "You

sound like our mother. Didn't you have enough of her lecture this past weekend?"

"I've been thinking about it. Mom's only after our happiness, and to tell you the truth, my instincts say Lauren likes you. She must like you if she's folding your boxers and ironing your shirts. I'm your brother and *I* don't even like you that much."

"Gee, thanks."

Justin gestured with his right hand. "You know what I mean. I really believe you should take another look at Lauren. Maybe in that beyond-a-friend way."

Jeff eyed Justin skeptically. "Is this just a ploy? You know, get me hitched to get Mom off your case? Although, come to think about it, maybe it's just the opposite. You seem pretty interested in Lauren yourself all of a sudden."

"Why wouldn't I be?" Justin countered with a magnanimous shrug. He'd expected Jeff's deflection. "I have to say that I have a vested interest in Lauren. It's obvious that she likes you as more than a friend, and if you marry her, she'll be my sister-in-law. Part of the Wright family. So of course I'm interested. None of us want a Mona the Bad again."

Jeff scrunched his face at the mention of his former college girlfriend. "Let's not drag up that memory. I'll admit, she was a bit on the psycho side."

"That's an understatement. The girl had commitment written all over her, and I mean the white suit, not the white dress kind. Anyway, compared with Mona, Lauren's a dream. You should give her a chance. Ask her out on a date. Do something besides laundry or *Monday Night Football*. It's Christmas. Holiday magic and all that. Go shopping. Buy her a piece of jewelry or some flowers. Eat at an expensive restaurant or do something romantic like skating at Steinberg."

Signaling his desire to end the conversation, Jeff lifted the laundry basket. "I don't think I feel that way about her."

Justin made an exaggerated stretch. The way to play Jeff was to plant the idea and let him contemplate it for a night or two. Just one more final push. "How would you know? Have you ever considered dating Lauren? Why don't you mull it over tonight? Better yet, dream about it. Think of her wearing nothing but black lingerie."

That put a painful memory in Justin's head and he winced. "You think about it, Jeff. I'm tired and I'm going to bed."

"What about the work you had to do?"

"It can wait," Justin said. His brother didn't need to know that that was a little white lie. Buddy jumped up onto the breakfast bar and began to purr. Justin looked at him. "And by the way, tonight you can keep the cat."

ONCE INSIDE his bedroom, Jeff finished putting his laundry away and within moments had settled himself down in his bed. Using the remote, he turned on the TV so that he could watch one of the late talk shows before he fell asleep. Seconds later his cat had curled up on his chest. "So, did you miss me?" Jeff asked. As usual, Buddy simply blinked, purred and then closed his eyes.

No, the cat hadn't missed him, but Lauren had. Jeff sighed, the movement of his chest shifting the cat slightly. Buddy opened one eye and gave Jeff an irritated look before making himself comfortable again. Although the cat was finally settled, the situation with Lauren wasn't. Jeff had been aware of her attraction to him for a while, which was one problem he didn't quite know how to solve.

Deep down, he felt that Lauren's feelings were misguided. She didn't love him, not with passion. To her, he was safe, comfortable, a buddy and a pal. That meant she was settling. As for *his* feelings, he'd thought about them already. To him, Lauren was like a sister. He loved her, but not in a passionate sense. And despite Justin's suggestion that he consider Lauren romantically, Jeff didn't need additional time to think about it. He knew his feelings. They weren't going to change.

While the most heroic thing to do might be to talk to Lauren and let her down easy, and he had been increasingly aware that he had to do just that and soon, Jeff had dreaded hurting her. He was privy to her dating history, and how many guys had declared that they only wished to be friends. Besides, as much as she decorated, the holidays really were a hard time for her. She'd discovered Mike's affair one week before Christmas.

Telling her how he felt and letting her down now would be like sticking a knife in her back. But, Merry Christmas, Jeff; another option had just now presented itself.

There could be no denying the room had exploded into fireworks the moment Lauren and his brother were together. She challenged Justin—got right back in his face. Yes, Lauren wasn't a pushover, which meant she wouldn't be one of Justin's usual simpering women. Lauren wouldn't put up with one inch of Justin's proverbial stuff. In Jeff's opinion, his brother could use a woman like that.

As for Lauren, she really couldn't do any better than Justin. Just look at his loyalty to his family. Justin also wasn't a playboy—well, not anymore. Two and a half years ago he'd loved and lost, and massaged his self-image with a steady diet of bimbos who told him what his fragile ego had needed to hear at that time. That had lasted about a year, then stopped. Justin then became choosy, and for the past year had chosen no one at all. After all, there were worse things than being alone. One was heartbreak. Yeah, that was the real reason Justin never went out with women who might somehow make him care, might make him vulnerable. Deep down, Justin Wright didn't want to get hurt. For all Justin's flaws, when he loved, he loved deeply and truly.

As did Lauren. And Jeff knew that Lauren didn't want to be hurt, either.

Now all Jeff needed to do was place Justin and Lauren together long enough so that they could fall in love and live happily ever after.

Besides, if he could get the two of them together it would benefit not only them, and of course he did have to admit that he had selfish reasons. First, a transfer of Lauren's feelings from him to Justin would solve the problem of potentially hurting her feelings and thus destroying his and Lauren's friendship. He valued that friendship; he didn't want to lose it.

Even better, a Lauren–Justin combo would get Jeff's mother off his case.

But best of all, it would benefit two people who probably needed each other more than they knew, two people who deserved to be happy and in love.

Matchmaking had never been Jeff's specialty, but it was Clint's. Clint had been instrumental in getting Jared and his wife together. Jeff resolved to talk to Clint first thing in the morning. After setting the TV's timer, Jeff drifted off to sleep, a satisfied smile on his face.

Chapter Five

Monday, December 13, dawned a perfect day and stayed that way. A good omen, Lauren decided. She needed one. Ever since Jeff's return from Buffalo, nothing had quite felt *right*.

Sure, she and Jeff had returned easily to their routines. Justin had remained his surly self and questioned every business decision and micromanaged every business move she made. But despite this normalcy, there was something intangible, something Lauren couldn't quite put her finger on, that permeated the air. Even the Christmas lights springing up on lawns all over St. Louis did little to cheer her. Something was amiss.

Now, as she finished the last touches of her makeup, applying it the way Meredith had shown her, Lauren decided she really had no clue what that something was. She glanced at herself in the mirror. The last time she'd worn her makeup like this had been only a week ago, that disastrous Monday night she'd tried to seduce Jeff and wound up with Justin, instead.

An event that she would not repeat tonight.

Maybe her unease was just her nerves. Galas such as tonight's chamber of commerce Christmas party and awards ceremony always made her a little tense. It was being held at the ritzy and beautiful country club of St. Albans, and Lauren knew that half the people attending the event would be wearing outfits costing more than she made in a month.

A knock on her doorjamb caused her to turn. "You didn't answer your front door so I took the liberty of coming in. I figured you were dressed. So how do I look?"

Lauren's breath lodged in her throat as Jeff stepped into the master bedroom. The huge mirror gave her a reflection of two views of him in his custom tuxedo. "Great," she said.

He did, too. The black fabric set off his strawberry-blond hair, making him even more handsome.

"Cool." Jeff gave her a wide grin in the mirror. "I hate these monkey suits."

"Penguin suits," Lauren automatically corrected, suddenly finding herself a bit disappointed that Jeff hadn't mentioned anything about her shimmery spaghetti-strap gown. She closed the powder compact and dropped it into the matching evening bag. Wearing her favorite red evening dress, she was as ready for tonight's events as she'd ever be.

"Whatever you call this god-awful thing," Jeff said, still referring to the tux, "I always feel like a waiter or a pallbearer when I wear one. I wouldn't have even bought this getup if I hadn't needed it for Jared's wedding and seen on *Queer Eye for the Straight Guy* that renting a tuxedo is passé. Then there's Justin. He wears these suits as if he'd been born in one. For all I know he was. He did arrive ten minutes ahead of me. Can you believe that he owns two tuxedos? *Two?* As if he could wear them both at once."

She didn't want to think of Justin. Even after a week the memory of his kiss still haunted her. Worse, she'd discovered that her heart had fluttered a few times when she'd seen him here and there at work, and that being in proximity to him still had the power to make her blush. She wondered when the embarrassment would cease.

Jeff glanced at his watch. "Speaking of Justin, you know how he hates to wait. You said you'd only be a few minutes when I called you earlier."

Lauren smiled and resisted the urge to give a little twirl. It wasn't often she got this dressed up. "I'm ready."

"Great. I'll drive." Jeff was already halfway through her condo. Lauren followed him.

"Your driving sounds good," she said. She reached the coat closet and pulled out her long wool coat. No fur, fake or otherwise, for her budget.

"Yeah, I like taking the car out," Jeff said. "Too bad

we don't have the time to drive Highway T past the bridge. I guess it is dark, though."

Jeff held the front door open for Lauren. She paused for a moment after she passed through.

"Maybe we could go this weekend. Eat at that restaurant in Labadie," she said. She liked the sound of that idea. Of course, having Jeff confined to the car with her after an event was always nice. Maybe for once she'd get up the nerve and kiss him. Maybe tonight.

She pushed the sudden image of Justin's kiss out of her head. She didn't need that now!

Jeff reached behind him and pulled her front door shut. "Hmm. That might be an idea. I'm not sure about this weekend, though. I've got poker Friday night, and don't we have the office Christmas party Saturday?"

For a moment she'd forgotten about that. "Yes."

"Maybe another time, then. Come on, let's not make the boss angry. My brother can be a real pain."

The drive from their condo complex in Creve Coeur to St. Albans took forty-five minutes. Just before Highway 100 wound down to one lane, Jeff turned right on Highway T and floored the gas pedal.

"I always love this stretch," he said, accelerating the Nissan 350Z sports car past the posted speed limit of fifty-five miles an hour. Dark farmland sped by as the car ate up the three miles to the entrance of the country-club community.

"I always like the houses in here," Lauren said. Besides the villas, most houses sat on at least an acre lot and many overlooked the Missouri River.

"Become a millionaire and one of them can be yours," Jeff said. "That's what they cost, a million on up."

"You're a millionaire," Lauren pointed out.

"Almost a millionaire, but I'd never want anything so ostentatious. The car is about my limit and the reason I bought it is that it looks cool and goes fast. When I modify it, it will go even faster. Now, Justin, he's a different story. The guy craves space. He's got a three-bedroom home in an older section of Chesterfield just for him. It's twice as big as my place. What a waste."

"He'd probably say that about your car," Lauren observed.

Jeff laughed. "Nah. He'd only complain about my overt need for sports-car flashiness. The base price for that 2004 Caddy CTS-V he just bought is fifty thousand dollars. Just because it has four doors doesn't mean anything. That car's got a Corvette engine in it so it's pretty darn fast itself, even gets to sixty miles an hour about a second before this one. Well, until I modify it. Then I'll leave him flat. Of course, my brother Mr. Corporate would never sacrifice business class for a two-seater, and being Mr. Frugal, he bought at the end of the year to save money. Here we are."

Within minutes they had found their seats at the Wright Solutions table of eight.

"You're sitting on that side," Clint said as they approached. Lauren noticed that Justin glanced at his watch, but his frown lasted only a second.

Her own frown, however, she had to quickly mask before it could become a permanent fixture on her face. Clint had to be holding out the wrong chair. She'd expected to sit by Jeff, but instead she and Jeff were seated directly across from each other at the round table.

"Have any trouble finding it?" Justin said as he approached.

"No," Lauren replied. Across the table Jeff was already in deep conversation with Clint. "Jeff knew where he was going and he really likes the road."

"That's good, I guess. He does love that car. Well, I guess this is my seat. Let me help you with yours."

"Thank you," Lauren said.

As he did the chivalrous thing and pushed her chair in, Justin accidentally brushed her shoulders. Immediately, tingles shot down Lauren's spine and goose bumps spread over her arms. Her breasts suddenly ached, as if remembering the feel of his hands just one week ago. She reached down and practically lifted the chair herself in an attempt to get away. "I'm fine, thanks," she said.

A silence fell between Lauren and Justin while the rest of their tablemates arrived and took their respective seats. When Justin shifted his attention elsewhere, Lauren used the time to compose herself.

Deep calming breaths, she told herself. *All I need are*

deep calming breaths. It does not matter that Justin Wright is sitting right next to my arm. We are colleagues. Nothing more. No one knows what happened. I will not think about how it felt when he kissed me. I just need more deep calming breaths.

Unlike that fateful night when the whole disaster that now was her life had started, this time her yoga training helped, and she calmed herself without anyone noticing. Desiring a drink of water, she stretched her right arm and reached for her glass. Her fingers connected with something hard, firm and definitely not glass. The ensuing sensual shock was not from the condensation collecting on the outside of a cold glass.

Her face flushed and she snatched back her hand, her fingers instantly cooling at being disconnected from Justin's warm hand. So much for deep calming breaths. At this rate, it was going to be a long evening. "Sorry," she said.

Justin's grin didn't quite reach the dark emerald-green eyes that studied her. "No problem. I always hate trying to figure out whose stuff is whose."

Mercifully, he broke the connection between their gazes and glanced around the table. "I think everyone is going to the left."

Lauren assessed the situation for herself. Jessica, the office manager, who was seated to Justin's right, lifted her glass to her lips. She'd definitely gone to her left.

"Yes, it's left." Lauren used her left hand and collected her water goblet. "Again, I'm sorry. I should have looked first."

"Really, it's okay." And with that, Justin shifted so that he could catch the conversation between Jessica and Clint.

The cold water sliding down Lauren's throat did little to quench the heat still diffusing through her. No, despite Justin's reassurances, it wasn't okay. She sat less than twelve inches from Justin's firm body, a body that had left a permanent sexual imprint on her brain.

She knew the feel of his fingers, the silky feel of his hard chest and the sensual feel of his chin when she'd planted passionate kisses on it. Jeff's earlier assessment of his brother had been dead-on. Whereas Jeff looked good in a tux, Justin looked great. He *had* been born to wear it, and the aura that the suit created accented Justin, making him almost larger than life. He could rival the late Cary Grant for charm, grace and poise.

No, sitting next to Justin Wright and accidentally trying to pilfer his water goblet was not okay. She'd touched him, and that brief touch had had the power to send wanton sexual sensations shooting through her.

Worse, besides the way the men wore their tuxes, Lauren's touch had confirmed another clear difference between the two brothers, a very obvious difference. Touching Jeff never sent any sensations rushing to Lauren's toes. In fact, just tonight when he'd helped her into his low-slung sports car and his arm had been on hers she'd felt nothing. Nada. Zip. Zilch. Purely platonic. Boring.

How come she couldn't get a rise from touching Jeff? She loved Jeff. They were good together, got along wonderfully. They never fought. They hardly ever even disagreed. She contemplated the paradox as the waiter arrived with their soup. She should be able to feel some magic spark, some hint of desire when she touched Jeff. But she didn't.

Instead, she felt the sizzle with Justin. Justin, the man who riled her in more ways than one, and not all of them good.

To be on the safe side, she made sure that when Justin passed her the rolls, she avoided touching him as she caught the opposite end of the basket. Concentrating so much on not touching Justin, Lauren hardly tasted the delicious lobster bisque. She resolved to do better with the salad the waiter was now placing in front of her.

Despite her discomfort with Justin's proximity, Lauren managed to smile and make the best of a delicious dinner. She'd chosen beef tenderloin in a red wine sauce instead of the chicken entrée, and the accompanying glass of Merlot had added a nice finish and mellowed her a tad. Without realizing it, somehow she'd eaten everything on her plate.

"Good?" Justin asked.

"Excellent," Lauren replied. "And I saved room for dessert."

His eyes twinkled and Lauren found herself wanting to immerse herself in those dark green pools. Wine. She never drank much, so she must have had way too much wine. That had to be the reason she found herself liking that she'd pleased him. She blinked. "What?" she asked. "Did you say something?"

He nodded. "I did. I said I like it when I'm with a woman who actually eats."

The wine she'd had with her dinner must have also loosened her tongue, for she said, "What, most women you know too afraid of you?"

He grinned as if she'd amused him. "Ha-ha. You're funny. No, it's just that they're too concerned about gaining an ounce. They'll order tons of food and pick at it. I often wonder if they devour what's in the take-out containers the moment they get home."

She'd never considered that before. "Maybe."

He reached for his iced tea. "At least you eat. And you certainly have nothing to worry about figurewise. That dress looks fantastic on you." His voice caught a little. "Red looks very, very good on you."

He'd noticed the dress. Lauren swallowed, her mouth suddenly bone-dry. She could almost feel Justin's fingers on her neck, but it was his emerald gaze that slid over her chin, down her throat and lowered to the V where the dress met her cleavage. She resisted turning her neck. How could a man make her react like this with only a smoldering glance?

"Yes, that dress ought to be outlawed," Justin added, his voice sounding even lower, huskier. "You've got quite a wardrobe tucked away in that bedroom closet of yours, don't you?"

Lauren took four deep calming breaths and a long sip of cold water. Neither did anything to quell the heat burning through her like wildfire. "And here I thought we were finally managing to have a real conversation," she said, her shaky laugh failing to hide that he'd gotten to her.

His eyes darkened and another illicit thrill shot through her heated body. "You and I both know that's not a dress for conversation. That dress makes a man want to know what's under it and what's not."

She struggled for the Lauren who could dish it out, the Lauren who could successfully match her wits against his. "Really, well, you'll just have to imagine, won't you?"

Instead of being brash and sassy, she sounded proactive and sexy, and Justin's darkened gaze lifted to catch hers. Lauren's breath lodged in her throat. "Trust me, I am."

Thankfully, at that very moment a waiter deposited a slice of cheesecake in front of her, giving Lauren an excuse to shift her body away from his as she reached for her dessert fork.

Saved by the waiter. Wasn't there a song in that or something? Justin thought. The bite of cheesecake melted in his mouth, but despite the confection's delicate texture, he had lost all sense of appreciation of the fine food in front of him. The only thing he could focus on was Lauren and that red dress she wore.

It should be outlawed. For tonight's gala, Lauren had chosen a simple, straight, red-sequined gown. The moment she'd shed her matching red jacket, he'd seen a lot more of her creamy white shoulders than he needed to. The spaghetti straps made him remember the merry widow she'd worn. She'd done her makeup differently from how she'd worn it at the office, tonight having applied it the way she had last Monday night. He'd fingered those honey-colored strands of hair.

His mouth had dried at that thought, making his last bite of the delicious cheesecake taste papery. He turned over his cup, and within moments another waiter appeared and filled his coffee cup to the brim. Perhaps some of the bitter black balm would help assuage his nerves, but as the master of ceremonies took the podium to announce a few end-of-the-year awards, Justin somehow doubted it.

To Justin's delight, Wright Solutions won three awards, including Jeff's commendation as most innovative chamber member for his computer-programming skills.

"Congrats," Justin said again as Jeff returned to the table. "We should have invited Mom."

Jeff grinned as he held up his plaque. "Nah. She's bad

luck. Every time she comes to any award ceremony, I lose. I'll bring this by tomorrow and show her."

"You better, or she'll have your hide," Justin replied.

"Yeah, and that won't be fun," Jeff agreed.

After that the music began, and people were free to dance and socialize.

Justin felt Lauren brush up against him as she stood. So much for being thirty years old, Justin thought. All Lauren had to do was barely touch him and his body immediately responded. By now he should be able to maintain some semblance of self-control. Once she was away from him and their table, he was safe to watch as she approached several award winners and offered her congratulations. He smiled to himself. Despite his constant questioning of her decisions in the office, in the field the woman was a natural PR goddess.

Hell, she was a goddess, period. That floor-length red gown hugged her body, reminding him of curves he'd caressed and kissed. Even after a week, she remained the proverbial siren. Perhaps coming without a date tonight hadn't been a good idea. Not that he'd wanted to take anyone in particular, and the Wright Solutions table was full. But anything would have been better than watching Lauren all night and knowing he couldn't ever touch her again. Watching her was starting to become absolute torture.

"She's great, isn't she?"

To Justin's displeasure, he realized Jeff had caught him staring at Lauren.

"She's a great hire," Justin made his voice noncommittal. "I have to admit I had my doubts when you told me to consider your neighbor for the position. She's a natural and a good fit for us. You could do worse."

Jeff drank his iced tea before speaking. "We've had this conversation already and so could you."

As Justin opened his mouth to speak again, Jeff quickly cut him off. "Don't even go there. I don't want to hear it. But you need to hear this. In the interest of company harmony, be kind to her tonight and ask her to dance. She thinks you hate her."

"She does?" Justin eased the shock out his voice before Jeff caught it. "Why would she think that?"

Similar green eyes contained absolute seriousness as they looked at Justin. "She really didn't indicate why. My own opinion is that you intimidate her. You grill her ideas more than you would if they'd come from Clint, for example."

Justin's defense was automatic. "I do not."

Did he? His forehead creased as he processed Jeff's assertion. The more he thought about it, the more he knew he did.

Jeff, however, shrugged. "You may not. I'm just telling you what I've concluded. She's never said anything directly to me. It's just a gut feeling I get from having been her friend for so long. Now that she's here, I want to keep her around the company for a long time."

"Well, there's one way you can definitely do that, and that's to get off the stick and marry the girl," Justin said.

"Not a right solution," Jeff quipped. "Give it up, matchmaker. Lauren's not for me. But we should keep her around the company."

"Okay, that's one thing that I agree with you on."

Jeff nodded. "Good. So be nice to her tonight. Dance with her. Tell her what a good job she does. Show her you're human and not some evil ogre."

That didn't sit quite right and Justin fingered the handle on the coffee cup in annoyance. "My brother giving me advice?"

Jeff lifted his iced-tea glass. "Yeah, well, this is Lauren. I know her."

"You should be working on knowing her better," Justin said.

"I won't even dignify that with a response," Jeff said with a grin as he stood and walked off, glass in hand. "See ya, bro."

Justin wasn't surprised to see Lauren dancing in Jeff's arms a few minutes later. But for some reason, that sight wasn't at all acceptable. Was this how the knights of old felt? Looking but not touching? Chivalry be darned.

Justin felt like stomping his feet, charging across the floor, sweeping Lauren into his arms, carrying her somewhere private, ripping that provocative dress right off her and making long slow love to her until both of them fell into satisfied satiated sleep.

If only he hadn't kissed her! The kisses between them had been more powerful than a blow to his solar plexus, and now it was all look and never touch again. What was that adage—never taste what you can't have to eat or you'll only crave it forever? If only that night hadn't happened. If only…

Justin pushed the if onlys out of his mind. The night had happened. However, unlike what he'd promised Lauren, he couldn't just purge it from his mind. He noticed her slightly flushed face as she and Jeff returned to the table. Well, for the sake of company and family harmony, he might as well make the best of the miserable situation. His brother had asked. Justin stood, made sure his tux was perfect and bit the bullet. "Lauren, would you like to dance?"

UPON HEARING Justin's words, Lauren froze. Did she want to dance? She felt Jeff nudge her in the back. Okay, if Jeff wanted her to dance with his brother, did she really have the option of saying no? Sure she did, if she didn't mind making herself look like a total idiot.

"I'd be happy to dance," Lauren said. She remained still as Justin rounded the table and approached her. Now that he was standing, his tuxedo created the image of his being a bit broader, perhaps a bit more powerful and more debonair than usual. Her mouth dried and she reached for her glass of water. She took one last bracing sip.

"Shall we?" Justin said as he offered his hand to her.

"Yes." Lauren placed her hand in his. Try as she might, she couldn't ignore the sensations caused by her hand being enfolded in his. She couldn't ignore the way her knees trembled as he led her out onto the dance floor.

It was only their history causing her to feel this way, she rationalized, only that buried night once again rearing its ugly head. Perhaps she needed to cleanse her soul by simply telling Jeff what she'd done, telling him exactly what had happened. Surely they'd laugh over it. Maybe her confession would finally quell the butterflies in her stomach.

"Ready?" Justin asked as the music began.

No! I'll never be ready to touch you again! "Yes," Lauren said, instead.

Long ago, Jeff had told Lauren that his mother had insisted all her boys take ballroom-dancing lessons. His mother was a wise woman. Jeff had danced divinely. But his dancing didn't prepare her for Justin's.

The band began the number, this time a slower waltz than the one she'd shared with Jeff. Justin drew her closer, and as she entered his personal space Lauren stumbled. Instantly, Justin gathered her close and held her tighter.

Never had she felt so clumsy, but Justin didn't seem to notice. He simply drew her even closer, so that if she moved forward slightly her head could lean on his chest.

His hand, now resting on the small of her back, sent tingles to her toes. She attempted to relax, to make her step sure. Neither spoke, this silence awkward yet somehow strangely comfortable as the waltz music flowed through their bodies and they moved in rhythm.

"Justin! I thought that was you." A high-pitched female voice cut through the music, and the woman accompanying the voice detached herself from her elderly partner.

As she headed in their direction, Lauren felt Justin's fingers tense on her back, and instantly she tried to pull away. Instead, Justin held her tight, his movement ending any escape.

"Hilary. Nice to see you again," Justin said.

The woman laughed. "I know. I was surprised. I thought Wright Solutions avoided these things."

Lauren stared at the woman. Was this one of Justin's former flames? She could be. Bleached-blond hair turned up into a chignon, blue eyes hidden by large luminous eyelashes that had to be fake, a figure to die for—yes, probably an ex.

Lauren considered pulling away, but as if sensing her impending flight, Justin intervened and inched her closer. "Lauren, this is Hilary Schuster, partner with Jenson and Sons. Hilary, let me introduce you to Lauren Brown, public relation guru. Wright Solutions couldn't exist without her."

The woman's blue eyes widened. "Really? You replaced Clint?"

"No, of course not," Justin said with a shake of his head. "But the company is growing so fast that we expanded our PR department. Lauren's one of the best hires we've ever made."

Was she? Lauren stared at Justin. His expression indicated that he was absolutely serious. A sense of pride suddenly filled her, and this bolstered her confidence as Hilary sized her up in a nanosecond. "I see. Interesting. Good for you, I guess, but disappointing for me. I had so looked forward to having more of your PR work directed my way."

Lauren's tension eased a sliver. That was right. Jenson and Sons had been Wright Solutions' PR firm before they'd hired her. Whoever this Hilary was, she wouldn't be around.

"Nope, we've taken everything in-house," Justin said. "Lauren buys whatever print we need. She's saved us a bundle and found some great advertising venues that have already paid off."

The music ended and everyone took a moment to clap for the orchestra. "Well, I really shouldn't keep you," Hilary said. "I already ruined enough of your dance as it is."

"Oh, it's fine," Lauren said hurriedly.

"It was nice meeting you," Hilary said in reply. "Good to see you again, Justin. Tell Clint to give me a call."

"You can tell him yourself. He's here somewhere," Justin said, but Hilary had already disappeared into the group of people now beginning another waltz, her black gown fluttering behind her.

Justin didn't let go of Lauren; instead, he turned her toward him. He tilted his head and smiled at her. "Sorry about that. Hilary always was the bold one. Shall we have another go?"

Lauren shook her head. Being in his arms was heaven, but being in his arms raised too many questions—questions she didn't want to even begin to think about, let alone answer. Now that the dance was over, she resolved to get out of his arms. "No," she said simply.

To her relief, Justin accepted her one word answer and without reply led her from the dance floor. As they walked along the perimeter of the room he said, "She's not my girlfriend, you know."

Lauren glanced over at him. "I didn't ask."

As it had earlier in the evening, his gaze became wicked and teasing and laugh lines formed around his eyes. "No, you didn't ask, but you were thinking it."

She stalled while they stopped at the bar. After she asked for another glass of water, she turned to him. "I was not thinking it. Who you date or have dated is none of my business."

His eyes still twinkled. "Admit it, you were. My hands were on your back. I felt every vertebra in your spine tense. And very nice vertebrae they are, too."

Lauren *had* been thinking it, and she knew he knew it. "Okay, it crossed my mind. That's all."

Satisfaction crossed his face, but not the type that was at her expense. "The complete story in a nutshell is that she and Clint liked each other a while ago, but it fizzled. Something about her going back to her ex, or maybe it was something different. All I know is that she hurt him, and I don't like seeing my friend hurt."

"I try to stay out of office gossip," Lauren said. To guide her through a thin space, his fingers touched her arm. She quivered. He cared about his friend and hadn't given Hilary any information. He did have noble qualities.

"All that happened before you came aboard, but the bottom line is that she wasn't my girlfriend." He seemed to be proud of the point. Because he was behind her, she couldn't see his face. "I'm not quite the playboy you make me out to be."

"I never said…" Lauren began. Her face heated and she was suddenly glad he couldn't see hers. "I did call you that. I apologize. I was out of line."

"No harm done," Justin said.

By this time they had reached their table and he drew abreast of her. Lauren scanned the room, but there was no sign of Jeff. Clint approached, a fresh glass of red wine in his hand. He passed it to Lauren. Unsure why, she set it on the table. "Thanks."

"Thought you might need it. I've got some bad news.

Jeff had an emergency page. He had to go straight to the client."

Lauren felt Justin's body coil next to her. "Which one?" Justin asked.

"Mendetech," Clint answered. "He told me to tell you both not to worry, that he'll see you sometime late tomorrow afternoon. If this is an all-nighter, which it sounds like it's going to be, I'm sure he'll want to sleep in."

"He usually does," Justin said. "I just wish he'd come gotten me."

"You were dancing and he didn't want to interrupt," Clint said. "And don't forget, he's a first responder. This is what he lives for."

It was, and Lauren knew it. Jeff enjoyed the thrill of racing the clock to repair any given computer crisis. Although she knew he was off doing what he loved, disappointment filled her.

She'd wanted to have another dance or two with Jeff. She'd wanted the ride home, the time alone with him. She'd wanted time to figure out why she didn't feel wild sensations with him the way she did with Justin. She'd wanted to at least talk, to perhaps somehow tell him what she'd felt and why her feelings were now starting to seem a bit misguided. Instead, she now needed a ride home. "I need a—"

"Jeff's one step ahead of you," Clint said. "He knows he stranded you and begged me to ask you to please forgive him and tell you he'll make it up. Don't worry. I'll drive you home. I've got some people to see first, but after that we can leave whenever you're ready."

"Forget it." Justin cut Cliff off and turned to Lauren. The intensity in his gaze startled her and she swallowed. Maybe she did need that glass of wine, after all. "You live in the opposite direction, Clint. Lauren, I'll be more than happy to take you."

Chapter Six

From bad to worse. That was the only way Lauren could describe the current situation.

"Great," Clint was saying, a look of relief crossing his face. "Thanks a lot, Justin. You're a pal. I wouldn't mind, but I heard that Hilary's here and she's unattached."

"She's here and I'm not sure whether she's attached or not," Justin said.

"Well, I aim to find out," Clint said. "You know what they say—once a fool, always a fool."

"Be careful," Justin said.

"I always am," Clint replied. He gave Lauren a knowing grin. "Lauren, you should be fine with this guy here. If he gets out of line, you just tell me. I can still take him."

Mortification filled her. This was not the end of a date. Justin was her boss and she was his employee. That was all. "We'll be fine, I'm sure."

"Great," Clint said. He clasped his hands. "I love

Christmas parties, don't you? Some spiked eggnog and some mistletoe and just maybe Hilary will melt." With that he left them.

After a few seconds of watching Clint's receding back, Justin broke the awkward silence. "I'm sorry about your plans," he said.

"Don't worry, I had no plans," Lauren replied.

The corner of his lips tilted upward. "Sure you did," Justin said. He reached forward and slid a forefinger under a red spaghetti strap. The simple caress of his fingertip sent heat pooling lower and she willed herself to remain perfectly still. "A seductively hot dress, a long drive home. Please. You certainly can't tell me that you didn't have some ideas for how to extend the evening and get what you want."

"Don't be ignorant," Lauren said.

"I wasn't trying to be ignorant," Justin said. He removed his finger, and held up his hands in a gesture of surrender.

"Yeah, right," Lauren said, her shoulder oddly missing his touch. "Try again. I wasn't born yesterday."

"I'd hope not. You're perfect the way you are. That dress…" He trailed off as his gaze slid lower. When he spoke again his voice came out even huskier. "If it was me you wanted, I'd peel that dress down to your waist the moment we got into the car. You're like a Christmas present, Lauren. Like the most tempting package just begging to be unwrapped."

Her body sizzled from the spark in his words. No! She hated Justin Wright. Hated his attitude, hated his womanizing, hated that his mere touch reduced her to a quivering, wanton woman. "Yes, but I don't want you," she somehow managed to say.

He gave a short, bitter laugh. "Yeah, no kidding. And my brother is an idiot. Let me know when you're ready to go home. I see some people I need to talk to."

With that he strode off, his exit leaving her physically shaken. Lauren grabbed the wineglass Clint had brought her. Liquid courage sounded good right now. Her hand shook and she only had a small swallow before she put the glass back down.

She suddenly felt exhausted and had no desire to stay any longer than necessary. She glanced across the room to where Justin stood talking to a couple. The woman said something and he laughed. Lauren's throat ached and she swallowed. Nerves. He'd reduced her to uncontrollable nerves. Her feet felt wobbly, but she managed to walk over to him. He arched an eyebrow at her. "I'm ready to go," she said.

He turned his head to the right as if in a half shake. "George, Claire, it's been great seeing you again. I apologize, but I'm Lauren's chauffeur home." His gaze narrowed slightly and he studied her. "Are you okay?" he asked. He guided her toward the foyer. "You look a bit pale."

"I'm tired," Lauren said honestly. Crawling into her

bed and sleeping the night away sounded like the perfect remedy for whatever ailed her.

"You've been working too hard," Justin said. "Wait here while I go get the car."

"That's probably it," she agreed.

Justin's Cadillac still had that new-car smell, and Lauren sank into the soft black leather, closed her eyes and luxuriated as they rode to her condo complex in silence. He pulled into the driveway and stopped close to the garage door. Jeff's condo was totally dark.

"I'll walk you to your door," he said.

"I'm fine," Lauren said, although in reality she wasn't. Her head pounded. Wine hangover, she decided. Justin was already opening his car door, and the need to stop him compelled Lauren to say, "I don't want your help. I do this every day. I'm a big girl."

But he climbed out of the car anyway, and was thus there to catch her when her ankle wobbled and her heel twisted underneath. Despite the cold December air, momentary warmth from Justin's arms steadied Lauren, soon to be replaced by the ice-cold wind that made her teeth chatter when she detached herself from being pressed next to his chest.

"Thanks," she said. Her body suddenly ached as if she'd been trampled on. She fumbled for her key. Justin took them from her, his firm hand covering hers.

"You're cold. Let's get you inside." He unlocked her door and opened it.

Lauren squinted as a pain shot through her forehead. She crossed the threshold and held out her hand. "Thanks again for the ride. I've got it from here."

"Of course you do," Justin said. He placed her keys in her hand and stood there a moment. Then, with a sharp nod, he said, "Good night." He strode off, his coat snapping about his legs.

Lauren shut the door and for a moment pressed her back against it. She was almost too tired to move. The pounding in her head increased. She grimaced. This was no wine hangover. But no way could she afford to have a cold. Not with the company Christmas party this Saturday.

Some acetaminophen and a good night's sleep and she'd be fine. Just fine.

"Hi, Lauren." Trisha, Lauren and Clint's secretary, paused in the doorway before entering Lauren's office. "You forgot to draw your secret Santa last week. I've got your name right here. Sorry for the late notice, but I had that nasty flu and this slipped my mind."

"Don't worry about it." Lauren managed to smile without wincing. Despite taking two acetaminophen caplets at 8:00 a.m. and two ibuprofen tablets two hours later, she still felt horrid. "I've got plenty of time to buy a gift before Saturday."

"The Christmas party should be fun. Everyone's talking about it. We're all really excited about dressing up for once and eating something besides nachos."

"Thanks," Lauren said. She took a long sip of water from the bottle on her desk. Her throat had been sore most of the morning.

Trisha placed the small envelope on Lauren's desk. "Not to be rude, Lauren, but you don't look well."

"I'm not," Lauren said.

"Hopefully, it's not the flu," Trisha said. "It's terrible this year. You did get your shot, didn't you?"

Shaking her head made it pound. Dumb move, Lauren thought. "I can't get the shot. They're egg-based and I'm allergic to eggs," Lauren said. "But I don't get sick. My body's too tough. I can't even remember the last time I was ill. Maybe high school."

"That's good," Trisha said. "Oh, I sent those party invoices to Accounting. Justin should sign the checks today."

"Great," Lauren said. "And you called the hotel and gave them our final head count?"

"Done," Trisha said.

"Great," Lauren said. Her chest burned suddenly, as if breathing hurt.

"Well, I'm off to lunch."

Lunch. Lauren hadn't eaten anything since a banana at breakfast. "I'll e-mail you if I need anything."

"Sounds good." Trisha disappeared with a wave.

After she left, Lauren dug in her purse for a cough drop. She was sucking on it when Justin entered her office, carrying a sheath of papers.

"Lauren, got a minute?"

No. "Of course," she said.

"I've been reviewing these party bills. We budgeted for party favors?"

"Yes," she said. Despite the cherry-flavored medicine in her mouth, she coughed.

"We're buying champagne flutes for everyone with our company logo and the party date?"

"Yes," Lauren said. She winced and reached for her water.

He frowned. "Why? Who approved this? I don't want some glass that won't match anything in my house."

Lauren's headache worsened. "Most people are bringing their spouses. They'll have a pair in their house."

"They're a waste of money," Justin persisted. "We already doubled the budget for this year's party so you could hold it at a hotel. Did we really need to spend almost a thousand dollars on party favors?"

Lauren rubbed her temples. "Yes, we do. You gave everyone mouse pads last year, Justin. Tacky and cheap. And it'll be a bit more than a thousand dollars when I'm done. We're filling the glasses with little scrolls that have twenty-dollar gift certificates to a local mall. Very tasteful and very appreciated. This is the time of year you let your employees know you value them. You don't give them a dumb mouse pad."

"Most of our employees are getting Christmas bonuses of company stock."

Justin changed tactics, but Lauren had that angle covered, as well. "Yes, and they'll love that. But at a party you give out something besides a mass-produced mouse pad."

"We're a computer company!"

Lauren stood. Her whole body ached from completing the ordinary movement. "No kidding, Justin. Everyone knows that. They don't need a mouse pad to tell them. Listen, I'm sick of you always questioning my every decision. I'm well within my budget on all of this, so just do me a favor. Stop being Scrooge, just sign the checks and…" Lauren couldn't finish her sentence as she began to cough.

"Are you okay?" Justin came around the corner of her desk.

Lauren bent over and covered her face with her hands. "I'm fine," she managed to say when the coughing ceased.

"You don't look fine. You look terrible." Justin set the papers on her desk and reached for her hand. "You're burning up."

She pulled her hand away. "Thanks for your concern, but I'm a big girl. I can take care of myself." Lauren coughed again.

"Yeah, and you're doing a super job," Justin said. "You need to go home. Rest. Drink lots of fluids."

"You are not my mother and I have too much to do. It's just a cold." Her body trembled and she wished she'd brought her sweater.

"Haven't you been reading the papers or watching TV? There's a flu epidemic. They even had a map in this morning's edition of *USA TODAY*. What's your temperature?"

"I don't know. I don't have a thermometer at home. I'm never sick, so why should I need one?"

He put his hand on her forehead. For once, his touch felt cool. "Well, you have a fever, and that means you're sick. I may not be your mother, but I am your boss. I'm ordering you to go home."

Lauren resisted the childish urge to stomp her foot. Justin was right, but he didn't need to know that. Frustration filled her. "Look, Justin, I have urgent press releases to finish. I'm not going home." As Lauren finished making her stand, she began coughing as her body struggled for breath.

"Stubborn, defiant." Justin struggled to contain himself from crossing the line. "Don't you realize you're ill? You're as white as a sheet."

"I'm always white," Lauren said. "I don't tan no matter how much I'm in the sun."

The room swam and she shuddered. Oh, how she wished he'd leave. Okay. She was sick. But she certainly didn't want the annoying Justin Wright to be one up on her. He was bad enough already as it was. The last thing she wanted to hear him say was, "I told you so."

She was tired of fighting with him and her body ached. "Look, it's my lunchtime and I've got an appointment after that, so if you don't mind, I'd like it if you left my office."

Justin didn't move. "Lauren, you're the one who needs to leave. You need to go home. You're sick." He raked a hand through his hair. "God, I wish Jeff were here. He's the only one you listen to, although only God knows why. Do I have to go to the Centers for Disease Control Web site and print out the flu-symptoms chart for you? You are the most stubborn, infernal woman I know."

Lauren coughed yet again. The cough was dry, but she couldn't stop it. She pressed a hand helplessly to her chest. Dear Lord, no. "Move," she said, but already her voice was failing her.

"No," Justin said. He crossed his arms. "I'm not moving until you tell me that you're going home to take care of yourself. You're extremely sick."

"Please move!" And when he didn't, Lauren took no satisfaction in proving him right as she threw up on his shoes. Instead, she stared, mortified.

Justin stared at his shoes, then Lauren. She tried to keep from gagging again. "I'm so…"

"Sick," he finished for her, although no satisfaction laced his voice. "And your apology isn't accepted until you get home. Are you going to concede now that you've ruined my shoes?"

"I'll pay for them," she said.

Justin grabbed some facial tissue on Lauren's desk and gently wiped her mouth. He then handed her her water bottle and she took a drink while he used more tissue to wipe up his shoes. He stood again and tossed the used tissue in the trash can. "I don't care about my shoes. Don't worry about them. Now, get your coat. No arguments."

Lauren simply nodded and Justin helped her into it. Even with her coat on, she was cold.

"You're shaking," Justin said. He guided Lauren from her office and toward the elevators. The receptionist glanced up as they approached her desk. "Lauren's sick," Justin said. "I'm taking her home. Call Maintenance and have someone come clean up her office."

"Will do," the woman said.

Within moments, Lauren found herself in Justin's CTS sport sedan. The Wright Solutions building was located in St. Charles County across from the Missouri Research Park, and soon Justin was pulling onto what the natives called Highway 40. It took him barely five seconds to hit the sixty-mile-an-hour speed limit.

As they crossed the Daniel Boone Bridge into St. Louis County, Lauren closed her eyes. She only got a few moments of peace before the car exited the highway. When she opened her eyes, she could see that Justin was turning left onto Olive. He could reach her condo this way, but staying on Highway 40 to Highway 270 was faster.

"The highway won't be crowded this time of day," she said.

Justin made a right turn less than a mile later. "I'm taking you to my house. I have a thermometer there and I want a new pair of shoes."

He made a few more turns.

"You were taking me home. I want to go home," Lauren protested.

Justin pulled into the driveway of a well-kept ranch home. The sixteen-foot garage door slid up automatically. "I said 'home.' I didn't specify whose. And mine is closer. Besides, you probably don't have a thing in your condo that would help."

A fit of coughing stopped Lauren from arguing back. Within moments, Justin ushered her inside.

Lauren had never seen Justin's house. She'd recognized enough of the neighborhood to know from the mature trees that the house was probably at least twenty years old. The aroma of new varnish assaulted her nose and she sneezed.

"They promised me the smell of my hardwood floors will disappear by spring, but I'm not inclined to believe them," Justin said. "In here."

He guided her through the house and into the master bedroom. The color scheme was green and burgundy. "The bathroom is right through there." He drew the comforter back and held it open. "In bed now."

She made one final attempt to keep herself on an

equal footing with him. "Gee, is this how you seduce all the girls? Brute force?"

Justin shot her a look. "I'm going to get the thermometer."

Lauren slid off her coat and stepped out of her shoes. She'd worn comfortable knits to work, and as she debated fighting Justin one last time to take her home, exhaustion claimed her. His oversize pillows appeared too inviting and she climbed into his bed. Deep down she knew she wouldn't win anyway. The man was a royal pain. But perhaps a wise one.

When Justin came back with the thermometer, Lauren was already fast asleep. He placed a hand on her forehead and she didn't move. She was so hot. She coughed and rolled over.

TWELVE HOURS PASSED before she woke up, right around one in the morning. Although asleep in the guest bedroom, Justin was by her side within seconds.

"How are you feeling?" he asked. He placed a hand on her forehead.

"Miserable," Lauren said. "My head hurts, I ache all over and my throat burns."

"My best friend is a doctor and he says you've got the flu that's going around. While you slept I had a whole lot of medicine delivered. He also prescribed you an antiviral drug."

"I thought I had to go in for that."

"Shh," Justin said. "Don't look a gift horse in the mouth, to coin the cliché. Now, I've got a bunch of things you get to take since you're awake."

"Okay." Lauren was too exhausted to argue with him. Besides, perhaps it was a bit perverse, but she found herself enjoying having a solicitous and kind Justin Wright wait on her hand and foot. She'd never experienced this side of him. She took her medicine, sipped some chicken broth and soon fell back into a deep sleep.

The next time she awoke, it was still dark. Justin was again there to pump her full of medicine, feed her and put her back to sleep. He even had a soft old T-shirt and sweatpants for her to change into in the bathroom.

"I have meetings all day!" Lauren said as she crawled back into bed. "I've got to go to work."

"I'm canceling everything," he told her. "And I can work from home. You are going to get well. Why you always argue with me I don't know."

"Because you're so convinced you're right and you're not," she said.

"I am right," Justin said. "It's in my gene pool. Get used to it."

"No," she said.

He laughed, pulled the warm covers around her chin and turned off the light. Her exhausted body betrayed her, and before she could argue more, sleep claimed her.

The pattern lasted well into the following day and Lauren spent hump day sleeping it away in Justin's bed.

Her fever finally broke around five that evening, and as Lauren sat up she realized she felt a little more like herself. Her throat felt better and her muscles didn't ache as much. She reached for the water glass that Justin kept constantly filled at her bedside, and took a long drink before grabbing a tissue. She'd developed a runny nose.

"I see you're up," Justin said as he entered the bedroom. "How are you feeling?"

"Better. What time is it?" Justin had removed the alarm clock and taken it to the bedroom where he was sleeping.

"It's almost five-thirty. How does some wild-rice chicken soup sound?"

"Actually, pretty good," Lauren admitted. She coughed. The cough was the most annoying aspect of her sickness. Each time she coughed it felt as if someone was trying to pull apart her chest.

As was becoming habit, Justin pressed his palm to her forehead. "Much better. You've cooled down. Now, let's see if we can get some of the congestion and muscle aches to loosen. How does a bath sound?"

"Good," she said.

"Well, the tub's clean. I never use it. So let me start the water for you. I'll even put the space heater on so you'll feel like you're in Aruba or something." Justin disappeared into the bathroom and within a few seconds Lauren heard the water running.

After a few minutes, he came back and stood in the

bathroom doorway. "I took the liberty of having Jeff get you some clothes. He should be here about the time you're done. I don't know what he'll bring, but it should at least fit better than what you've got on now."

Lauren stared at Justin. Today he wore a chamois-colored flannel shirt and blue jeans. He'd cuffed the sleeves to avoid getting them wet and the unfastened top button allowed for just a peek at his chest.

"Thanks." As she stepped out of bed, she heard the doorbell sound.

Justin gestured toward the bedroom doorway. "That would be Jeff. I'll check on you in about fifteen minutes, okay?"

Lauren nodded and escaped into the bathroom. With the heater and the hot water, the room felt warm and steamy. She took off her clothes and, gratefully, she stepped into the tub. To create bubbles, Justin had used his shower wash. Lauren smiled when she saw the brand. She hadn't pictured Justin as a mild, soap-free guy. Then again, she hadn't pictured Justin Wright correctly at all.

She'd horribly misjudged him. He was a decent guy. Even that didn't begin to describe him. He'd been nothing but kind, gentle and absolutely perfect during her time convalescing at his house. As for his playboy reputation, both Justin's home and cell phones had been silent. He'd had maybe one call, and that had been from work.

Yes, Justin Wright surprised her. She'd never seen

a man so concerned with making sure she was comfortable. Even Mike, who supposedly had loved her at least in the beginning, hadn't been so thoughtful or wonderful.

She was vulnerable now. That was it. She wouldn't— couldn't—let herself see him differently. She'd already kissed him. Her body already craved his. Now he'd become Mr. Kind and Caring. No, the last thing she needed, especially in a moment of illness-induced weakness, was to fall for Justin Wright.

It was too late to leave tonight, but tomorrow morning she'd tell Justin that she could care for herself and insist that he take her home.

JUSTIN TOSSED OPEN his front door. "Hey, Jeff, did you remember to bring Lauren's bathrobe?"

"No," his mother replied. She brushed by him without invitation. "And before you give me my obligatory hello kiss, just why is your brother bringing you Lauren's bathrobe? And by Lauren, are we referring to Lauren Brown, his next-door neighbor?"

Justin leaned over and gave his mother a kiss on the cheek. It always amazed him that his mother, who was barely five feet herself, had given birth to twin boys who topped six feet. "You'd be waiting too long for the explanation I'm not going to be giving you," he said.

"Oh, I don't think so," Rose Wright said. She removed her scarf.

"Oh, I do," Justin said, catching the scarf. "So, to what do I owe this wonderful honor?"

"The way you treat me is shameful, just shameful. I should be greeted with wide-open arms, instead of an inquisition." She handed him her coat. "I stopped by your office today and you weren't there. So I came here. Well, I detoured by the mall first and did some Christmas shopping, and then, since you only live five minutes away, I came here. What is so wrong with that?"

"You could have called first?" Justin suggested.

His mother gave an empathic flip of her wrist. "You know I don't own a cell phone."

"I'll buy you one for Christmas," he said.

"Which is why I'm here. With your elder brother, Jared, on his honeymoon and not returning until January, it'll just be the four of us celebrating the holiday this year. Your father wants all of us to travel to Branson and spend the holidays with his family. His mother doesn't have many years left. I'm sure she'd love to see her favorite grandsons."

"We aren't her favorite grandsons. All we hear about is how we're not married, how computers aren't like running a real business and how well Garrett is doing in England. Oh, and we hear about how famous our cousin Cindy is since she appeared on that reality-television show where she almost snagged the bachelor. Of course, she's a granddaughter, not a grandson."

"Well, I can't help it that your father's side of the

family is certifiable. Thank goodness he's not like his brother Melvin. But I did marry your father for better or worse, and like it or not, his mother is your eighty-nine-year-old grandmother."

"You know Jeff will find some computer crisis to deal with," Justin said. "He hates those whole-family get-to-gethers. Besides, I don't think he's forgiven her for boxing his ears when he was five."

"But you'll be there." Rose looked at Justin for support. "I can count on you, right?"

"As always," Justin said.

"Wonderful," Rose said. The doorbell sounded again and Justin inwardly groaned. What perfect timing.

Without waiting, Jeff opened the door. "Hey, I've got a bunch of Lauren's things, even her bathrobe. How's she doing?" Jeff hadn't bothered with a suitcase, and he held a pile of female clothes in his arms. "Oh. Hi, Mom."

"Hi, Jeff." Rose glanced curiously around. "Would someone like to tell me what's going on here?"

Both twins began to speak at once.

"Well, Lauren got sick and…"

"Lauren got sick on his shoes and…"

"Lauren's staying here until she's better."

"Justin's dating her, so it's okay that they're living to-gether, even temporarily. Although I'm sure that'll even-tually change."

"I'm what?" Justin turned to his brother. He was dating Lauren? Surely he hadn't heard Jeff correctly. And

Justin knew exactly how his mother would interpret Jeff's words.

"You're planning on having Lauren live here permanently?" Rose asked.

His mother would interpret wrong.

"No."

"No? She's living here, but you're just toying with her?" Rose planted her hands on her hips.

Justin took a deep, calming breath. "I'm not even dating her."

Rose's lips puckered. "No, she's just needing a place to stay temporarily. Like I believe that one. Justin Wright, you're thirty! Not twenty! You know better than to string a woman along. I raised you better than this!"

Uh-oh. This was sliding downhill fast. "It's not like that. She's sick."

"Oh, don't tell me she's pregnant," his mother said.

The thought of Lauren pregnant, her body swollen with child—his child—made Justin pause and consider. The idea was oddly not repulsive at all.

"Don't worry, Mom. She's not pregnant. Yet." Jeff emphasized that last word with his trademark stir-up-trouble grin.

As Jeff said those words, Justin knew his twin only had a few more seconds to live. Jeff must have recognized the fact, for he dodged by him and his mother. "I'm going to put these clothes on your bed."

"No!" Justin lunged after him and just missed Jeff's

shirtsleeve. "Lauren's taking a bath. Put them in the guest room."

"She's in your bathtub? The one you never use?" Rose made a tsk-tsking noise. "Justin."

"She has the flu. Someone has to take care of her." Justin watched as Jeff disappeared from view. Thankfully, he heard his brother enter the guest room.

His mother stared at Justin curiously. "What's wrong with your brother taking care of her? She lives right next door to him."

"And when has Jeff been of any use to any woman except to fix her computer?" Justin said. "Lauren got sick at work and I brought her here."

"Oh." Rose's face fell and Justin knew she'd already been envisioning the next Wright wedding. His mother was not one to let moss grow under her feet. "So you aren't dating her?"

"Of course he is," Jeff said as he reentered the living room. "Or he at least plans on it. He adores her. Don't you?"

Their mother visibly brightened. "Knowing that you were going to settle down would be the best Christmas present ever," she said. "Ever since Jared got married, I keep having this vision of lots of grandbabies. And, of course, then I'd have an excuse not to travel to Branson."

"We're all going to Branson for Christmas," Justin informed Jeff. After the grief Jeff had just dished out, Justin took some perverse pleasure in wiping the smug smile off his twin's face.

"We're all spending Christmas Day with Grandma Hilda? When did all this come about?" Jeff asked.

"This week, and yes, we are," Rose said. "It would mean a great deal to your father. His mother is almost ninety. She's old."

Jeff exhaled sharply. "And she's too mean to die. She'll probably outlive us all."

"Jeff," Rose admonished.

"Well," he said, cocking his head as though daring his mother to contradict him. Rose remained silent for a moment as if contemplating her next move.

"I need to check on Lauren," Justin said. Afraid of what yarns his brother would weave the moment he left the room, Justin edged toward the hallway.

Jeff gave his brother a wicked grin. "Go. We'll be fine here without you. We'll want to know how she is when you return."

"Oh, yes," Rose said. "I do like Lauren. She's such a nice girl."

Unable to divide himself in half and be two places at once, Justin gave up and entered the master bedroom. "Lauren?" he called. He walked to the closed bathroom door. "Lauren?"

No answer. Using his knuckles, he rapped on the door. "Lauren?"

Still no answer. Justin stepped back from the door

and drew a hand though his hair. Now what? He could tell the water wasn't running. Had she fallen asleep? He knocked again, this time even louder. "Lauren?"

She still didn't respond.

He stepped back from the door and paced for a moment. This should be easy. She should answer. He should not be wondering whether to barge in and risk seeing her in the tub.

He'd already felt her body. To see it as natural as the day she was born... He paused. No, that image wasn't right. She'd changed since the day she was born. While she still had that baby-soft skin, she now had curves that called to a man. Lots of them. Breasts that called for a man to cup them in his hands.

Justin groaned as a lower part of him flared to life. This was not what he needed right now. He banged again. "Lauren?"

Still no answer. That decided it. He had no choice. He was going in. She would not drown in his bathtub.

He turned the knob and it yielded easily; she hadn't locked the door. He gave a brief sigh of relief as he inched the door open. "Lauren? Lauren, are you okay? Lauren?"

The warm, humid air assaulted him. "Lauren?" From the doorway, all he could make out was the top of her head, so he stepped all the way in. "Lauren?"

Still no answer.

He muttered a curse word and walked across the

floor. "Hey, Lauren. How are you doing? Feeling any better?"

The heat rising from the water in the large garden tub brought small beads of perspiration to his forehead. "Lauren."

She had to be asleep. That made the most sense. But what did one do in a situation like this? Ever since that night when she'd tried to seduce his brother and had gotten him, Justin felt he hadn't been able to make one correct move around Lauren Brown.

He averted his head and stepped toward the tub. Slowly, ever so slowly, hoping she'd say something, scream at him even, so then he could stop, he turned around so that he could completely see her.

She was indeed asleep. She was indeed naked. She was indeed beautiful.

Justin's groin tightened. He needed to move away. He needed to leave, go get some pots and pans from the kitchen and then, from the safety of his bedroom, bang them together to wake her up. But he couldn't move. His feet hadn't rooted—they'd disappeared. No messages from his screaming brain got through.

Instead, his lower half ruled. He simply stood there and stared like a hungry man outside a bakery window. A fine film of soap covered the top of the water. Long gone were the fluffy bubbles that would have concealed Lauren fully. Instead, the tips of her breasts peeked above the water. The shadow that lay at the juncture of her thighs showed teasingly beneath the milk-white soap.

Her breathing was even and relaxed, as if her sinuses had finally cleared.

His breathing was ragged and painful, as if he'd been punched in the chest. Dear Lord. If she wasn't sick, if she were his woman, he'd climb right in there with her and make passionate love to her.

His brother was an idiot and sure as hell did not deserve a woman of Lauren's caliber.

Not that Justin deserved Lauren, either. Right now he was lower than dirt, standing their and enjoying a sight he should never have been privy to.

He should never have kissed her that night. He should never have felt her body, felt the desire in his body that hers had roused. No, everything between him and Lauren was wrong, wrong, wrong. He wanted her, but didn't have a chance.

Fate was mocking Justin Wright.

Somehow, Justin managed to get his feet to move and he edged back toward the door. The last thing he wanted now was to somehow wake her and be caught as a Peeping Tom.

He knew how Sir Gawain felt. Chivalry wasn't easy. Chivalry wasn't fun. But, like Sir Gawain, it was his code and it was all he had.

Trying to be as quiet as possible, Justin shut the door behind him.

Chapter Seven

The click of the door made Lauren start. "Justin?"

She came awake in an instant, the sudden movement sending a sharp pain through her forehead. She winced. "Ouch."

She rubbed her temples and then stirred the water so that its heat spread throughout. The water's warmth was heavenly. Her chest felt much better and her muscle aches had lessened.

She must have imagined the noise. She'd been asleep, dreaming of… She frowned. What had she been dreaming of? Deciding it didn't matter, she let her hand trail through the water. Her condo didn't have a huge garden tub like this, and she was determined to make sure her next one did. In this tub, she could soak without either her knees or her feet popping out of the water. Everything fit.

She glanced around and decided that Justin probably had left the room "as is" when he'd bought the house.

Crisp white bead board ran about halfway up the walls and ended with a one-inch shelf that ran the perimeter of the room. The top half of the walls was painted a robin's-egg blue. Fluffy white towels adorned the chrome towel bars and fluffy white bath mats covered the white floor tile. Even the cabinets were white. The room had an aura of the seashore without gaudy sand and shell motifs.

She stretched again, pointing her toes, then flexed them to loosen her tight calf muscles. The water was beginning to get a little cold and her skin had started to pucker. As much as she'd have loved to linger, it was time to get out.

Lauren stood and grabbed one of the huge white bath towels. She wrapped herself in it and stepped onto the bath mat. The heater's warmth kept her from getting a chill. She toweled off and looked around. She'd folded her dirty clothes and put them on the counter. She really didn't want them back on and she didn't have her bathrobe.

Her gaze fell on the dark blue terry-cloth robe hanging on the door. Surely Justin wouldn't mind. She'd already taken over his bed, borrowed his clothes and used his tub. What was one more imposition?

She slid into the robe. Since Justin was six foot one, his robe fell way below her knees. She belted the robe as tight as possible and slowly opened the bathroom door. "Justin?"

The bedroom door was ajar and she could hear voices in the living room. She paused. Jeff was here. The last thing she needed was for him to see her like this. She walked to the door. "Justin?" she called down the hall.

"Lauren?"

Hearing footsteps approaching on the hardwood, she ducked back into the bedroom and tugged on the belt just to be certain it was still tight. "I'm in here," she said.

He pushed open the door but didn't step inside. "Are you out of the tub?"

"Yes. I'm decent."

Upon hearing those words, Justin entered the room. Her face flushed when she felt his gaze on her robe-clad body.

"Did I hear Jeff's voice? Did he bring me some clothes?" she asked.

"Uh, yes. He did. Hold on. I'll get them." Justin made a hasty retreat and Lauren frowned. She touched her hair. Only the bottom few inches were wet so she hadn't wrapped it in a towel. It still probably looked pretty bad, though, given her illness.

Justin came back bearing an armful of clothes. He laid them on the bed. "My brother doesn't know how a suitcase functions. When he travels, he tosses everything in a duffel bag and uses the iron at the hotel. I'll lend you one of my suitcases when you're ready to go home. Ah, here's your robe. Not that you don't look charming in mine, but this might be more comfortable."

He came over and held it out to her. Lauren took the

robe in both hands. "Thanks," she said. "Look, just leave the stuff. I can put everything away later."

Justin shook his head. "No. You're not supposed to exert yourself. Just tell me what you want and I'll leave it out," he said, starting to put things on hangers.

He'd set his jaw stubbornly. Arguing with him right now wasn't worth it. "Please, just put it all on the dresser," Lauren said.

"But what do you want to wear now?"

"That nightgown will be fine," Lauren said.

Watching Justin handle her clothes in such an intimate manner made her uneasy. Sure, she and Jeff did laundry together all the time, but somehow, seeing Justin handle her things was different, much more personal.

As she'd asked, Justin set everything on the dresser and held up the Lang flannel gown that she'd been wearing the night after her failed seduction.

"Hey, I remember this," he said. He grinned. "I still like the other outfit better. So, do you really like wearing these granny gowns?"

Lauren's face heated at the memory of her seduction gone awry. "Jeff gave it to me and it is comfortable," she said. She reached for the floral flannel, the robe gaping slightly. She grabbed at the lapel with her free hand and attempted to hold it closed. "I'd like to get dressed."

"Oh." For just a moment Justin appeared flustered, and with a sharp movement of his arm he thrust the gown at her. "Sorry. How about I go start the soup? Are you hungry?"

The fabric felt soft under her fingers as she snatched the nightgown from him. "You know, soup sounds good. Didn't you say wild rice or something?"

Back on safe, secure ground. "Yes. Wild rice and chicken. Get dressed and climb back in bed. I'll bring it to you."

She shook her head. "No. I'd like to be out of bed, even if it's just for a few minutes. I'll feel like I'm getting better. Really."

He didn't appear too convinced. "Are you sure? I don't want you to have a relapse."

"Yes, I'm sure," Lauren insisted. Could he not get a clue and leave?

"If you're sure." With that, he finally turned on his heel and quickly disappeared.

Lauren clutched her nightgown to her chest and took it back into the still-warm bathroom. She shed the blue robe and eased into the gown. For the first time, she questioned Jeff's gift. Justin certainly wouldn't have bought her a granny gown. Jeff, who viewed her as a pal, had.

Deep in her heart, Lauren knew the truth. Even if she'd shown up at Jeff's and he'd been there, instead, he probably would have raced to cover her up with a bathrobe or a blanket.

His feelings didn't go beyond friendship. She was probably lucky he had been sent to Buffalo. Justin's embarrassment had been bad enough, but he'd wanted her. Jeff never would and his rejection would have been pure humiliation. At least now that would never happen.

Still, by wearing the gown, did that make her prematurely prudish? She was twenty-eight, not eighty-two. Maybe she should buy herself some sexier sleepwear. But for right now the gown was warm and concealing, so Lauren pulled her own robe tight around her waist a few moments later.

Now all she had to do was brush out her hair and she could finally face Jeff.

JUSTIN'S HOME had been remodeled once, and in addition to carving out a wonderful master bathroom, the former owners had expanded the kitchen. What had been a simple arrangement between two walls had been opened up into an L-shape featuring a breakfast bar.

When Justin entered the kitchen, he found his brother sitting at this bar, a bottle of Justin's best imported beer in his hand.

"Hey," Jeff said. "Mom left while you were in with Lauren. She said she'd call you later—she was running late for dinner with her sorority sisters. You know how they always meet at P. F. Chang's once a month. They love that place. Anyway, as for the beer, I got thirsty."

Justin rolled his eyes. *"Mi casa es su casa,"* he quipped, saying in Spanish, "my house is your house."

"Besides, it's not like you don't know how to help yourself. You're good at that."

Jeff shrugged. "What can I say? At my age a man learns to do two things well—forage and fend for himself."

"Speaking of fending for yourself, just so you know in advance, you're dead."

Although Jeff knew exactly what his brother meant, he still cocked his head and shot Justin a dubious look. He drank some of his beer before asking, "Dead?"

"Dead," Justin repeated. He opened the lazy Susan cabinet, took out two small cans of wild-rice chicken soup and set them on the counter. "I don't know the time or place, but you will die. I can't believe you told Mother I'm dating Lauren."

Jeff shrugged. "It made her happy. Did you see her face? It was already Christmas for her. Besides, how else were you going to explain the fact that Lauren's living here?"

Justin arched an eyebrow. "By telling the truth? That Lauren's sick? That she's not living here, just staying until she's well?" he said.

"She's been here two days. She's living here, just like you lived with me while your floors were being redone."

Justin mentally counted to ten as he set the oven at three hundred fifty degrees. He reached into another cabinet and took out a cookie sheet. He had some of that canned biscuit dough in the refrigerator. "Trust you to split hairs," he said.

"It's my job," Jeff replied with a salute of his beer. "And did you see how happy Mom looked?" he said again. "I tell you, Christmas is coming up."

"She was already planning the wedding." Justin raised the wooden spoon he'd just retrieved and waved it at his brother. "I swear, one day I'll kill you," he reiterated.

Jeff shrugged. "I'd haunt you from the grave and guilt would make you go insane like that Edgar Allan Poe character. You know, in 'The Tell-Tale Heart.' It would be kind of cool, I could come back from the dead like Madeline Usher and—"

"That's a totally different Poe story, and just out of curiosity, when are you planning on going home?" Justin opened the cans of soup and poured them into a saucepan. "There's not enough here for three."

"Gee, you're certainly hospitable, and it's not as if you couldn't open another can. Don't worry, I'll leave right after I make sure you haven't abused poor Lauren." Jeff pushed his empty bottle on the counter.

"I have not abused poor Lauren," Justin said. He busied himself placing the biscuit dough on the cookie sheet to keep his idle hands from strangling his beloved brother. "I've made sure she's had everything she's needed and…"

Jeff held up his hands in surrender. "Gee, I was joking. You certainly are defensive. Methinks just a little too much so. Yeah, all this stuff about Lauren really has you going. Back to that conversation we had a week ago. What *is* going on between you two? Let me guess—you like her."

Justin put the cookie sheet in the oven and straightened. "I do not."

Jeff had the gall to laugh at him. "I think you do."

"You are nuts."

Jeff shrugged as if being labeled crazy was of little consequence. "So? I've known that since birth. After all, I've had to grow up with you and I'm related to Uncle Melvin—that's enough to make me certifiable. Anyway, I think you're frustrated because you've got Lauren in your bed and you can't do anything with her. All looky and no touchy. No wonder you were trying to foist her on me. You're falling for her yourself!"

Justin had already done something with her, and the memory of caressing her satin skin caused him to redden. Jeff noticed Justin's flush. "Ah-ha! I'm right!"

Justin covered with a counterattack. "You don't know anything. You're so blind you don't realize the girl is in love with you. You should go out with her."

Jeff shook his head. "Lauren and I are friends, that's all. I think you should go for it. You have my total and complete blessing."

"I think you should mind your own business."

"Oh, listen to that defensive tone. What? Can't handle the thought of seeing Lauren outside of the office? Too chicken? Or, ooh, I get it. You've already tried, haven't you? Yeah, that's it. You've already tried and she shot you down."

"I haven't tried," Justin said, his irritation rising. "If I did, she wouldn't shoot me down."

Jeff's expression said it all. "Uh-huh. Mr. Confident and Cocky rears his evil head. No, the more I think about it, the more I'm certain you aren't nice to women. You've been nicer to Lauren more than anyone else I can remember, including your prom date. You must really want something from Lauren if you've got her staying here with you. You know, buttering her up or something."

"I do not want anything from her." Justin didn't understand why he was even having this argument with his idiot brother. How had matters and this conversation gotten so far out of control? "Lauren has the flu. She got sick all over my shoes."

"So? Why didn't you just take her home to her house and tuck her into her own bed?"

"Because people with this flu should have someone care for them—" Justin drew a breath "—and you are incompetent."

Jeff didn't argue the second point but instead said, "Her mother lives in O'Fallon. That's certainly not the edge of the earth."

Justin opened his mouth and closed it again. Jeff did have a point. The soup began to boil and Justin turned down the heat.

"You didn't answer my question," Jeff said.

"And I'm not going to. This whole conversation is stupid. I can't believe that you're harassing me like this.

What's it to you? If you're so concerned about Lauren, you should be more than friends."

"Ooh, open hostility now. Why don't you just admit you want her? The last time I saw you this riled was when I came home and told you I'd gotten together with Betty what's-her-name after the homecoming game our freshman year in college. You blew a gasket because you wanted her, asked her out, you had a lousy date and then a few days later she got together with me. I'm just too much of a stud for you."

"This is nothing like that," Justin said.

"Right. So prove it. Show me that you don't want Lauren just because she wants me. Start by treating her right, and I mean really right. Take her on a date. A real one."

"We're colleagues," Justin said as he realized his brother had just turned the tables and boxed him into the proverbial corner. "Colleagues shouldn't date each other. It makes for bad office politics if things don't work out, not to mention a potential sexual-harassment suit waiting to happen."

Jeff shook his head. "You are worthless. You're afraid of her rejecting you the way Betty did! I know Lauren's had this thing for me, but trust me, it's you she wants."

"Women don't reject me. Betty didn't reject me. It was all a game to her. Date each brother or something. And Lauren isn't like that. Also, Lauren wouldn't reject me. Please. I told you, I haven't even tried to kiss her."

Well, okay, that was a big fat lie. Lauren had rejected

him quite well the night she'd stripped and seduced. And he had kissed her. But she had wanted Jeff, not Justin.

That was a lie Justin didn't see the need to correct, especially now that he knew his idiot brother wasn't even interested in Lauren.

Oh, how Justin wanted to shake Jeff and knock some sense into him. Couldn't the man recognize what a catch Lauren was? Even better, she was crazy about Jeff, enough to come over in a slinky little number that still made Justin's blood boil when he thought of it.

But Jeff couldn't see anything but his victory over his brother. "You know, I'm not going to buy this argument from you, Justin. If she wouldn't reject you, then you should ask her out. I'm going to tell Clint about this, and Jared when he gets back. Hell, you're a bigger chicken than our older brother was. At least he had the guts to go through with placing that personal ad. You're a chicken. Pure and simple."

Fighting words, and they both knew it. Jeff had pulled out the pride trump card and placed it out in the open. There was no way Justin could back down now. Not if he wanted to save face with the guys and thus stop what would be endless nights of ribbing during Friday-night poker games.

"I am not a chicken," he said between gritted teeth as he forced himself to unclench his fists in an attempt to relax and regain control.

"So you'll ask her out?" Jeff pressed.

"If it'll keep your fat mouth shut," Justin retorted, his attempt at control failing.

The timer beeped and for a moment Justin diverted himself from the annoying conversation by taking the biscuits out of the oven. His agitation had manifested itself in a hand that shook slightly inside the oven mitt.

"You'll see I'm right," Jeff said.

"Fine," Justin countered. "I'll ask her out. But I warn you, she won't reject me and you'll discover yourself not liking it much that I'm the one holding her, touching her and kissing her. And when that happens, well, don't you dare even think about crying to me that you were a fool and lost the best thing that ever happened to you."

"I doubt that it'll happen. I know Lauren. In fact, I don't even think you'd last a week with her," Jeff said.

"Really?" Justin said. He set the cookie sheet on a baking rack. The biscuits looked delicious, but he had no real appetite. "You don't realize how wrong you are. I'm not even going to bet you on this the way we used to do. I'm just going to rub your nose in it and tell you I told you so. You won't live it down and I can't wait."

Jeff made a noise that sounded like a dubious snort. "Sure thing, bro. Whatever you say. I'll believe it when I see it. Just invite me to the wedding, okay? I'll be your best man. How's that?"

At that moment Justin heard a shuffle of footsteps on the hardwood floors. To indicate to his brother that he should be quiet, Justin lifted a finger to his mouth. Lauren was coming down the hall. "We're in the kitchen," he called.

"Coming," she called back, and within a few seconds she entered the room. She wore her own robe and she'd brushed her hair. It fell around her shoulders, a few wet tendrils clumping together. Even devoid of makeup, Lauren had a beautiful face, and Justin suddenly wished he were the one she was holding her arms out to.

But it was Jeff, and already he was drawing her into a huge bear hug. "How are you, sickly one?"

"Not well," she said with a weak smile, trying to hide that she really didn't feel well at all.

"Must be my brother's cooking," Jeff said as he released her. "He's poisoning you, isn't he? Don't worry. If anything happens to you, I'll kill him. It'll give me the excuse I've been looking for all these years."

"It won't come to that," Lauren said. Justin heard an odd tone in her voice and his forehead creased as he tried to figure out what was wrong. She'd lowered her head to look at her feet—she wore a pair of his socks—and he couldn't see her expression. "I can handle Justin. Besides, up until now he's been pretty much a gentleman. You don't have to worry about me."

Jeff came around and grabbed a biscuit off the cookie sheet. He studied Lauren for a moment. "Yeah, I bet you can handle him. But you know I always worry about you. That's what friends do. Well, you two enjoy your dinner."

She appeared shocked, and Justin wanted to kill Jeff for putting that expression on her face. "You're not staying?"

"Not enough grub, and I really don't like wild-rice chicken soup anyway," Jeff said. He ate a bite of biscuit. "Before I came over here, I called Clint and he's meeting me at Dave and Buster's. I'm in a gaming mood." Jeff glanced at his watch. "Heck, I didn't realize how late it was. He's probably already there."

"Oh, okay," Lauren said. She looked crushed and Justin's blood boiled. "Well, we can catch up at work tomorrow."

Jeff shook his head. "No way. You stay here and rest up tomorrow. Give it at least one more day. The world of Wright Solutions won't end without you."

"I've got the Christmas party to finalize," Lauren protested. "There is so much I need to do. It's at a hotel for the first time and there are so many things that can go wrong. The party—"

"Will be just fine. It's not until Saturday night and these hotels know exactly what to do. I want you to rest so that you're not still staying here with this bozo on Monday morning. That is, unless you decide he's worth keeping or something."

Justin clenched his hands. His brother was pushing the limit with that comment.

"Jeff, I really have a lot of other work to do, as well, and—"

He touched a finger to her nose and Lauren stopped

speaking. "Get well, Lauren. Do it for me, okay? Promise me you'll take another day off and just come in on Friday. And for only a part of the day at that."

Bile swept through Justin as he watched the exchange. Lauren seemed like such an obedient puppy with Jeff and it made Justin angry. Lauren was full of fire, life. Heck, she fought him like a trouper. But with Jeff she simply nodded and conceded. "That's my good girl," Jeff said. "I'll see you Friday, let's say at around ten. You are not to step into the office a moment sooner. I will check up on you, you know."

With that, Jeff popped the rest of the biscuit into his mouth, gave her another quick hug and disappeared. They heard the front door shut behind him. Without Jeff's presence, the kitchen seemed bigger, and to occupy himself, Justin began to pour the soup into bowls.

"Hungry?" he asked.

He was rewarded with the sound of Lauren's stomach growling. "Actually, I think I am," she admitted.

"Great. Go have a seat at the kitchen table and I'll bring the soup right over."

Within moments he'd brought her a bowl of soup and a plate with two warm biscuits on it. "Tell me if you want more," he said as he went to get her a glass of ice water. "I made plenty."

Instead of replying, Lauren lifted the spoon to her lips and took a small sip of soup. He could almost see it travel down her smooth white throat. Did she know how pretty she was? Sensing his stare, Lauren said, "It's good."

Justin snapped out of his trance and grinned. "Well, I can't admit to making it," he said. "I'm not much good at cooking except to open a can or two or to boil some pasta."

"You have a great kitchen for cooking," she said.

Idle chatter. That was a good idea. He put away the pot holder. "Thanks. I like it. It's one of the things that sold me on the house."

"My kitchen is much too small, but then, I do have just a condo, not a house."

"Jeff always calls this my wasted space. I guess I wanted a house because it came with some ground to call my own," Justin said. "I don't like mowing the grass, but it gives me a sense of having accomplished something when I'm finished."

"Is that important to you?"

Her voice sounded odd again, almost far away. He didn't understand. "Is what important to me?"

"Having a sense of accomplishment. Achieving what you set your mind to."

He hadn't really spent hours analyzing it. "I don't know. Isn't that what everyone wants? To accomplish their goals, to achieve their hearts' desires?"

"Maybe," Lauren said. She broke off a bit of the biscuit and put it in her mouth. "But what if people get in the way?"

He was totally lost. "What do you mean?"

"Are your personal goals more important than theirs, or even them?"

"I don't think I follow you," Justin said. "If you mean, do I care about how my goals impact others, then of course I do. I'm not a bad guy, Lauren. At times you seem to think that I am—or at least, I get that impression. Probably because we cross each other so much at work. Maybe that's it. I know I'm a demanding boss."

"Yeah, perhaps that's it," Lauren said. "I was just curious, that's all. I probably shouldn't have pried."

It was suddenly important for him that she understand one thing about him. "You can pry all you want," he said. "If I want to answer, I will. If I feel it's not your business to know, I'll tell you. I don't mean to make that sound harsh. What it means is that if you have a question, you should always ask me, instead of playing guessing games. Don't let anything fester. Ask me. It's always better to have things out in the open."

Lauren pushed away her half-eaten soup. Her forehead creased, and Justin's fingers itched to soothe the ridges that had formed above her nose. "I think I want to lie down again."

"I knew this would be too much," Justin said. He felt like such a heel. "I should have brought you the food in bed. I should have insisted, been that demanding guy I'm supposed to be."

Her lips barely curled in a smile at his attempt at

humor. She stood. "It's fine, really. I'm just not as hungry as I thought. I'm sorry. You did go to some trouble."

"You're still really sick. Don't be hard on yourself. It was no trouble. Seriously. I opened some cans and dirtied some dishes. Nothing to feel guilty over. I'll just put the food away for later. Maybe you'll want to eat then. Come on," he said. "Let's get you back to bed."

Justin reached his hand out, but Lauren didn't take it. She simply followed him back to the bedroom. He lifted the comforter. "In you go."

Lauren slid back into bed and Justin pulled the comforter up to her chin. "You wake me if you want anything tonight. I'm serious about that."

She knew he was and so she nodded. "I'm fine. Really."

"Do you want me to turn on the TV? I can put in a movie if you'd like. And the remote's right there by your bed."

"You don't need to do anything," she said. "I'm used to caring for myself."

"You have the flu," Justin said. "I'm here to help. I'm worried about you. You're not in this alone. I've chosen to be here."

"I'm tired," she said.

The flu aside, she really didn't feel well at all. After Justin left the room, she climbed out of bed and headed into the bathroom to brush her teeth.

Overhearing Jeff and Justin's conversation had rocked her to her core. When she'd first come down the hall she'd caught Jeff telling Justin to take her out on a real date. Confirmation that Jeff didn't like her as more than a friend had been blow number one, but she might have been able to live with that mortification.

Then Justin had responded that he and Lauren were colleagues. To find out even *he* wasn't interested in her, after kissing her and letting her stay with him, was blow number two. Yet they were such adversaries that he shouldn't have liked her anyway. She thought she could live with that.

But then she'd heard Jeff call Justin a chicken, and Justin's reply that he'd ask Lauren out and would last longer than a week with her.

No wonder Justin was being so solicitous to her right now. Could she ever trust him again? She'd been questioning his early reputation, but now…oh, the shoe fit now. At this moment, he wore it well.

To be treated so casually! She'd talk to Jeff about this conversation later, when the time was right. She'd pull him aside and tell him what she'd overheard. They were friends enough that she could come out and say to him that his words had hurt her.

But Justin! Even though he told her to not let anything fester, she knew those were just empty words. He'd sworn he could make her fall for him. He'd said he could last more than a week with her!

What was it about men that made them bet on women? What was it that caused them to want to notch their belts with a woman's pain? How many of her own girlfriends had this same thing happened to?

Well, she, plain old Lauren Brown, would not let it happen to her. She would not let Justin Wright get away with this. She'd give him a week, all right. A week from hell.

She bit her lip hard to keep from crying, to fight back the tears that threatened to flow any moment. She'd fight him. She would. No matter how tired she felt. No matter how tired…

She finished brushing her teeth and started for the bed.

The room seemed suddenly unsteady and Lauren barely heard Justin call her name as the world tumbled into black.

Chapter Eight

Justin sat by her bed most of the night. Thank goodness he'd been walking into the room when she'd blacked out. He'd caught her and then called his buddy. His doctor friend had told him not to worry unless her fever spiked. Justin had held a thermometer under her armpit; it had read 99.2 degrees Fahrenheit. She had a low-grade fever, nothing serious enough to take her to the emergency room. After her collapse, he'd laid her on the bed and gently shaken her awake. She'd come around enough to mumble and let him know that she was, for the most part, okay. Then he'd covered her up.

In sleep, her body battled the next round of the flu. Justin felt powerless as he watched her cough. He watched her toss, turn and try to breathe. He heard her sneeze and sniffle and agonized that he could do nothing but turn up the vaporizer. He smoothed her hair from her forehead and traced his fingers over her face and hoped that she felt some comfort from his touch.

His own eyelids begged for sleep, but he fought them until well past three in the morning.

He slept little, for he was up every two hours so that he could check on her again. He left her only to make himself some coffee. She finally stirred around seven.

"Hey," he said. "How are you?"

"Better," she said.

He studied her. She did look better. She wasn't as pale, and her eyes seemed brighter. Relief filled him and he knew he cared, cared for this woman perhaps way too much.

"Good. I'm glad to hear that," he said. "I've set some orange juice on the bedside table. Here. Let me hand it to you. I'll also bring you some toast."

"Okay." Lauren accepted the orange juice and took a long sip as she watched him go.

It surprised her that she was so thirsty, but then, she hadn't eaten much dinner. She stared at the empty glass in her hand. How different the morning made everything appear.

She'd collapsed and Justin had apparently carried her to bed. She remembered his gentle touch. But she couldn't focus on that. She had to remember that Justin was only doing all this for his own reasons. He had an ulterior motive.

He was not the man she'd thought. Or was he? What man did all these things just to win a woman to save face?

She wished the answers to her questions were clear

as he came back a few minutes later carrying a dinner plate with two pieces of toast on it.

He handed her the plate. "I've buttered the toast already. Ah, I see you need more juice. I'll go get you some."

"Could I have some jelly or jam, too? If it's not too much trouble."

"Of course it isn't," he said. He went back to the kitchen and quickly returned. "I've brought both grape and strawberry. Do you have a preference?"

"Grape," Lauren said. She suddenly couldn't decide. Grape was her favorite, but it had been so long since she'd had strawberry. "No, strawberry. How about one of each?"

"Okay." As Justin proceeded to spread the jellies on the toast pieces, Lauren took a moment to study him. He looked exhausted. She'd never seen bags under his green eyes. Even his mouth drooped slightly. Guilt twinged her conscience. "Were you here all night?" she asked.

"I slept for a bit," Justin said. "But you were tossing and turning. I admit I watched you for a while. And I did have to take your temperature. I took it under your arm."

"Oh," Lauren said. He'd spent the whole night making sure she was okay. He'd even taken her temperature. All of a sudden self-conscious, she fingered the pearl-like buttons on the front of her flannel gown. Had he undone them? If he had, had he seen anything? And did it really matter?

Of course it mattered! He'd told his brother that she'd

fall for him. And she was! What woman wouldn't eat up this wonderful attentiveness and male sensitivity? Again she reminded herself that it was just a ploy.

But if it was only a ploy, his actions certainly went way beyond the call of duty. Shouldn't just staying with him have been enough? Justin didn't strike her as the type of man who would be so low as to pretend to care.

She dutifully ate the toast and tried to decide what to do. She wasn't the type of person who'd ever gone about teaching someone a lesson. She'd seen a movie like that once, but Lauren knew she didn't have the same personality as the character Kate Hudson played in *How to Lose a Guy in Ten Days.*

She couldn't set out to be the woman from hell. And Justin didn't look or act like the Matthew McConaughey character. Then again, Lauren hadn't known Justin had an agenda until last night.

She wasn't going to let him just walk over her. But what to do about it—that she wasn't sure about. Of course, the two adversaries did end up in love and living happily ever after at the end of the movie—

She looked up and caught Justin's gaze. "You're staring at me. Why?"

Justin's sheepish grin indicated that he didn't mind being caught. "Well, aside from the fact that you're beautiful, I guess I've been dreading telling you that I've got to go into the office for a few hours. I've rescheduled everything, but I have an overseas conference call that I can't cancel. Would you like me to bring anything back? Food? Clothing? Something besides office work, which I won't bring no matter how many times you might ask?"

And there was her answer. A way to make Justin pay, but in a semiharmless way that might be beneficial to him in the end. "Actually, I do have some concerns. You don't have any decorations."

Stunned, he blinked several times. "Decorations?"

Lauren nodded. "Yes. It's Christmas and you have no decorations. I'm finding it depressing to be sick and without Christmas spirit. At least Jeff has a small tree. If I'm going to be here a few more days, could you get some decorations? I mean, would you mind? I like the holidays more when there are decorations around. This is a hard time of the year for me anyway and your house is so bare."

"A hard time of the year?"

"I caught my boyfriend cheating on me at Christmas. We were living together, and…you know, I don't want to talk about it. Let's just say we had no decorations to split when we divided our stuff."

"I'm sorry to hear that. Decorations. Okay. I'll see what I can do. I want you happy, Lauren. I really do."

Lauren smiled and wished she could believe him. "They really aren't that much work. Get a lot. I mean, you need a tree and ornaments and everything else you can think of. And buy a few of those storage tubs for afterward. Don't forget stockings. You have a fireplace. You need stockings and those holders."

"Do I need a plate for cookies for Santa, too?" He laughed, and Lauren wondered if it was for real or just to impress her.

"Absolutely." Lauren's head hurt when she gave it a vigorous nod.

"Don't do that. You're wincing. Which reminds me, you need your medicines before I go," Justin said.

"Uh-huh," she admitted.

"I'll go get them and be right back. Eat your toast."

"Yes, boss."

Justin stuck his head back in through the door. She'd never seen a more serious expression on his face. "I'm not your boss, Lauren. Not here. Remember that."

With those words, he disappeared from view. Lauren rubbed her arms and mentally chided herself. She didn't need to have her heart race. She didn't need to get chills of excitement. She didn't need Justin Wright. All he wanted from her was to prove a point. Right?

JUSTIN FINISHED his conference call a little after eleven. He set the receiver down and looked around his office. He'd always liked it. Decorated in burgundy and green, dark manly colors that suited him, the room felt like one of those old-time law offices or classic libraries. His home was done in the same color scheme, reminiscent of an old-time men's club.

Jeff's office, by contrast, was stark, modern. He had minimalist furniture, and his color scheme was metallic black and white. His condo had the same feel. Except that Jeff had a two-foot-high Christmas tree.

Justin walked to the door of his office and looked out. Wright Solutions didn't have an executive floor per se, and just outside Justin's office were the sales cubicles. Even here Lauren and her secretary had gone to town. Tinsel hung from hooks on the ceilings. Christmas cards lined the partition walls. He couldn't remember Wright Solutions ever having such a happy holiday feel to its offices before.

The employees seemed happier and more productive this year. And his secretary had told him that almost all the employees had RSVP'd that they and their spouses were attending the office Christmas party. Maybe holding it in a hotel did make a difference.

Which made him a bah-humbug, modern-day Scrooge, because he still didn't like the idea. He also didn't like the fact that Lauren's ex had been such a jerk at Christmas. They hadn't even had decorations to divvy up, she'd said. Lauren deserved much more than to be treated like that. It was important for Justin that Lauren feel comfortable in his house. If that meant Christmas decorations, well, so be it. He walked the ten feet to Sylvia's cubicle. "I'm taking off for the rest of the day," he told his secretary.

She arched an eyebrow. "Is Lauren still sick?"

"Yes, and you know better than to listen to office gossip."

Sylvia shrugged. "Did I say anything? It's your business and hers where she convalesces. I just happen to like her and am concerned for her, that's all."

Justin's defenses rose. "I'm taking very good care of her. She should be in tomorrow. Anyway, I need to know where to get Christmas decorations."

"You want Christmas decorations?" Sylvia stared at him. "In all the years I've worked for you you've never even sent a Christmas card. Do you even know what decorations are?"

"Yes, Sylvia, I know what decorations are. I do have a mother. So just tell me where I can buy a tree."

"Real or fake?"

"Which is easier?"

Sylvia shook her head in disgust. "I assume you need ornaments, too?"

"Yes," Justin admitted.

"Why are you doing this? Is this all for Lauren?"

He bristled. "Even Scrooge had a change of heart."

Sylvia snorted. "I doubt ghosts came to see you."

"Fine. Not that it's your business, but Lauren has expressed that my house is a bit lacking the holiday spirit and she finds it depressing."

Sylvia nodded. "I don't doubt that."

Did everyone think him strange for not decorating? "Well, if it makes her feel better, then I'm for it. The flu is really pretty nasty and I want her well. So, where's the best place to shop?"

Sylvia rattled off the names of several stores. "You'll find everything you need at one of those places—just ask someone for help. Good luck."

"Thanks," Justin said.

Sylvia stared after him, then shrugged and turned back to the notes she was typing. She looked up only when she realized Jeff was standing in front of her. "Where's my brother?" he asked.

"Shopping for Christmas decorations," she said.

Jeff stared at her. "Did I hear you right? Christmas decorations?"

"That's what I said." Sylvia didn't have to be discreet with Jeff. He'd already recruited her for this matchmaking mission. "Lauren told him his house was a bit lacking."

Jeff chuckled. "A bit? That boy has no clue about Christmas. I don't believe that he's really going to let loose with some cash and get what he's always called useless frivolity. I have to say I'm impressed, Sylvia. I guess we're ready for phase two." Jeff whistled as he walked away. Sylvia simply shook her head and resumed her work.

AFTER TAKING her medications, Lauren dozed on and off the rest of the day. She did wake up and eat a little of the food Justin had left on a tray by her bed, but she was sleeping when Justin returned, his arms laden with shopping bags. Lauren had no idea he'd been in the house for a while until the thunking woke her up. The clock beside the bed told her it was almost three.

"Justin? Justin, is that you?"

She heard footsteps indicating he was on his way toward the bedroom. "It's me," he said, appearing in the doorway. Seeing she was up, he stepped inside. "How are you feeling?"

"Better. I slept most of the day and I did eat what you left for me."

He gave her a wide grin that sent a tingle to her toes. "Good girl."

"I heard noises. What's going on?"

He grinned again, wider if that was possible. "I dropped the Christmas-tree box. I'm putting the tree together now."

Lauren stared at him for a moment. "You bought a tree?"

"Yep. And ornaments and a whole lot of other things, including a wreath for my front door and one of those plastic things to hang it on."

"I don't believe it." He'd actually gone shopping at her suggestion.

"Believe it," Justin said. "It was actually kind of fun shopping for all this stuff. A saleslady who looked just like Mrs. Claus helped me out. So, do you want to help me decorate? You can issue the directions and I will follow your every command."

"You follow my every command? I'd like to see that." Lauren eased off the covers, angled her legs off the bed and put her feet on the floor, still wearing his socks. She winced. "Ooh. I'm pretty stiff from lying here all day."

He handed her her bathrobe. Their fingers touched briefly. "Then the exercise will do you good."

Lauren followed him out into the living room, and stopped and stared.

Besides the box containing the tree, there had to be at least ten to fifteen other large shopping bags around the room.

"Feel free to start digging through the bags. Just don't overdo it, okay?"

"Okay." It was Justin who'd overdone it. Lauren shook her head in disbelief as she looked first through the bags on the coffee table. These contained boxes and boxes of ornaments. Another bag was filled with bags of tinsel. Other shopping bags contained table runners, holiday dishes, candles, two stocking holders, two stockings, three nutcracker statues, a tree skirt and a small manger set.

He must have spent at least seven hundred dollars. Guilt began to eat at her. She hadn't expected him to be this extravagant. She'd expected him to buy a two-foot tree, tops.

"Like everything?" Justin asked. "As I told you, I had a saleslady help me. We had great fun. Everything coordinates. I saw this display I liked and I bought the exact tree and all the decorations with it."

"You bought so much."

He shrugged as if the money and the effort were of little consequence. "It'll make up for all the years that I didn't have anything. Besides, now Jeff can't lord it over me that he has a tree and I don't."

They spent the next two hours assembling the Christmas tree. After sorting the branches into piles according to size, Lauren fluffed and bent the needles before Justin clipped the branches into place. He'd purchased a seven-foot tree, and he'd had to move a chair out of a corner to make room for it. The tree came with prewired, multicolored lights, and he'd bought a shimmery star for the top.

They decorated the tree with red bows, red ribbons, tartan-plaid angels, candy canes and Santa ornaments. The tree, when finished, was beautiful.

"Like it?" Justin asked.

"I do," Lauren said. He'd worked so hard to make everything perfect and he'd succeeded handsomely.

"Oh, I found one other thing," he said. He lifted a four-inch-square box out of one of the bags. "When I saw this I thought of you."

He handed it to her. The white paper felt smooth to her touch. He gave her an encouraging smile. "Go on, open it."

Lauren's fingers trembled as she undid the paper. She fingered the red tissue paper, then peeled it back to reveal what Justin had brought her.

It was another Christmas ornament—an egg-shaped porcelain birdhouse complete with a small porcelain red bird sitting on a ledge above the doorway. The bisque-colored house had lattice windows trimmed in teal, and came with green-tissue grass inside. She put the box on the table and held the ornament up.

"It's beautiful," Lauren said honestly. She felt humbled. This was not the gift of a man intent on winning a bet. This was the gift of a man who cared. But that made no sense. Sure she was staying with him, but this gift said more than friendship.

"It was hand-painted by the artist. She was in the store while I was there. It's signed right here."

Justin turned the ornament around so that Lauren could see where it was signed and dated. "I love it," Lauren said. "I don't know what to say except thank you."

"I'm so glad you like it," Justin told her. "Come on. Hang the ornament on the tree. You can take it with you when you leave."

Lauren looked at the tree they'd spent such a long time trimming. "It doesn't match."

He shook his head. "That doesn't matter. It's not supposed to. Hang it on the tree."

"Okay." She grabbed an ornament hook and slipped it through the gold string loop on the birdhouse, and soon had her ornament hanging just a few branches from the top.

"There," Justin said, pleased. He smiled at her.

"You've got your own ornament. Feel better about staying at my place now?"

What she felt was more confused, but she couldn't tell him that. He'd bought her an ornament, one that must have cost a pretty penny. Plus, he'd spent tons of money on decorations.

She stepped forward—then stopped before she could follow through on her urge to kiss him.

Embarrassment and mortification consumed her. She had been about to kiss Justin. Sure, just a friendly kiss, but she had to remember Justin's words from the other night. He had practically made a bet that he could date her for more than a week.

"What else do we have left to do?" Lauren asked.

"These two bags," Justin said. "The manger and all the table decorations." He began rustling in the bag and came up with another square box. This one, though, wasn't a gift box. "I didn't think I'd bought that," Justin said.

"How could you miss buying a plastic mistletoe?"

"I don't know. You tell me. How about the fact that the saleslady went a little nuts, too?"

She tossed the box at him. "I'm sure some of your women will love an excuse."

He caught the box easily and opened it. He removed the mistletoe and looped the string over his finger so that the mistletoe swung freely. "I don't have any women. And if you weren't so sick and contagious, I'd dangle this over your head right now."

A thrill shot through her. "You wouldn't dare."

He stepped toward her. "Are you sure?"

She took a step back, her legs touching the coffee table. She was trapped. "Of course I am," she said, trying bravado.

"You're really, really sure about that? You're sure that I wouldn't hold this up like this…"

He inched even closer and held the plastic mistletoe ball out over her head. He smelled divine, so male and primal, and her knees weakened.

"It looks to me like you're wrong." Justin leaned forward, lowered his head toward her. "You see, I would dare."

His breath was soft on her cheek.

And then his lips lightly touched her cheek.

It was the gentlest of kisses, almost a whisper and a dream. Her cheek sizzled and she fought to steady her shaking knees. His breath tickled her ear as he spoke.

"When you are well and can breathe without coughing every few seconds, I'm really going to kiss you, until your lips can't take any more. I don't give a damn about your unrequited love for my brother. I'm going to kiss you until you don't even know he exists." Justin stepped back, his eyes hooded. "And I will, Lauren. Believe me, when the time is right, I will. That's truly no dare."

With that, he tossed the plastic mistletoe ball onto the sofa and left the room.

Lauren stared after him. He'd disappeared into the

spare bedroom where he was sleeping and closed the door behind him. She pressed her hand to her cheek. He'd told her he'd kiss her until she forgot all about Jeff. The intensity behind his words hadn't frightened her. Instead, it had made her warm and wanton. She wanted that kiss. God forbid, she wanted Justin Wright. She wanted a man who might only want her because, well, because by doing so he'd get his brother off his case.

It all came down to that. Or did it?

Could he really care?

Could he really want her for herself?

Because right now she wanted him. If that made her fickle, so be it. She and Jeff had always been pals, though, and she'd never touched him. Not once.

But Justin! Oh, her body still simmered just from looking at him.

The problem was immeasurable.

She had no idea what to do, or how to ignore the physical magnetism that was Justin Wright.

She needed to talk to Jeff. He'd put Justin up to this ploy. He'd know how far Justin would go. Yes, that was what she'd do. She'd start with Jeff.

Chapter Nine

Lauren set foot in the office at a little past ten, which was past the time she'd promised Jeff.

Jeff, however, wasn't in the office. He'd flown out at 6:00 a.m. and was in Chicago dealing with a computer crisis.

"He'll for sure be back for the office Christmas party tomorrow night," Sylvia had told her. "Don't worry."

And despite any desire to do otherwise, Lauren really didn't have time to worry, anyway. She dealt with the press releases that had to be approved. She dealt with last-minute party preparations. She dealt with Justin popping his head in every thirty minutes to make sure she wasn't overdoing it.

Before she knew it, it was three in the afternoon. Her only break had been the lunch hour Justin had insisted she take.

"How are you doing?"

By now so used to his appearance, she didn't even

bother to look up from her computer. "Like I said thirty minutes ago, I'm fine," Lauren said.

"So are you about finished?"

Lauren glanced around her office, deliberately glancing past where he leaned against the doorjamb. "Finished? There's no way. I have at least another three hours of work to do first."

Justin shook his head and straightened. He approached her desk. "Not tonight. You can come in on Monday and catch up."

A strand of Lauren's hair escaped and she pushed it behind her ear. "Look, Justin, it's sweet of you to try to be my keeper, but I'm a big girl and I can take care of myself."

"Okay, big girl. Try this one. I'm leaving and I'm your ride home."

She stood up and planted her hands on her hips. "Don't you even try that with me."

He grinned, his gaze wicked. "Don't dare me, Lauren. I think you and I both know what happens if you dare me. I'll let you have one more hour and then we leave. See, I'm not such a bad guy. I can compromise."

"Right," Lauren said dubiously.

Justin gave a magnanimous shrug. "Fine. Don't go with me. I'm sure you can give me that argument of calling a taxi and all that. However, because Jeff won't be back until tomorrow afternoon, I need to drop by his condo and feed the cat. So if you want to miss this chance to pick up your warm and fuzzy cow slippers, so be it. The offer's only valid right now. Going. Going…"

Lauren's mouth dropped open and she gave a squeak. The thought of seeing her condo, getting her mail and making her own choices of clothes was too tempting. "You jerk. You know I can't fight you on this one!"

Justin's smug smile said it all.

Lauren sat back down, her chair thumping against her back. "Cad."

"Yep, which is why you adore me. See you in one hour, darlin'." He drawled the last word as he left.

After he'd disappeared, Lauren allowed herself to smile. Although she knew he was serious about leaving in an hour, she'd enjoyed the lighthearted battle of wits. It was so different from his normal grilling. Almost that of two lovers teasing each other in their own private joke.

She'd just thought of Justin as her lover. Lauren surveyed her desk. She still had a mound of paperwork to go through. One hour? There was no way.

Having Justin as her lover would be easier than finishing all this.

She gave it her best shot, though, and managed to be ready when the ever-punctual Justin showed up again. He pointed to his watch. "Ready?"

"Ready," she said with a saccharine smile that told him that just because she was ready didn't mean she'd given up. "Just let me grab my briefcase and…"

Her gaze fell on the envelope she'd set aside Monday. She'd completely forgotten about her secret Santa. She needed to get whomever a twenty-dollar-or-under present. She grabbed the envelope and, without opening it, tossed it into her briefcase. When she closed the lid, a bunch of papers fell on top. Then she grabbed her coat. "Let's go," she told Justin.

They arrived at the condo complex about thirty minutes later. Lauren went inside her condo and Justin went to feed Buddy. Lauren didn't want to be in Jeff's condo with Justin. Even though she had been staying with him, the idea of being where the seduction had gone wrong didn't sit well.

She left her front door unlocked and then sorted through the mail that Jeff had stacked on her kitchen table. Nothing that couldn't wait until Monday. She glanced around what had always seemed like home. For some reason, her condo felt oddly empty, barren. She went into the bedroom and took out her garment bag. She just wanted a few more items of clothing, including a dress for tomorrow night's event. She dug into the closet. She'd had the red dress dry-cleaned. Should she wear it again? It was either that or her black beaded sheath. She had a feeling a lot of women would be in black. She'd go with the red.

Now to find something to wear underneath it.

Lauren paused for a moment. Did she dare? She heard the front door to her condo open and then Justin's voice. "Lauren? Hey, are you about ready? I'm hungry. Let's eat."

Oh, yes, she dared. She reached into her lingerie drawer for the fated outfit she'd bought for that "night." She'd finally been able to wash it and store it. Now she took it out and held it in her hands.

Justin Wright wasn't going to seduce her. He wasn't going to have his way or his week.

But she would make him want. She would make him suffer for his comments to Jeff, make him suffer for making her want him, the cad.

She grabbed the black lingerie and shoved it into a pocket of her garment bag. Then she grabbed a few other items and added them, as well.

Justin appeared in the bedroom door. "So this is the sanctuary."

"It is and get out," Lauren said, but he was already halfway in. He walked over and fingered the red dress.

"Good choice," he said. "So, are you planning on driving me crazy?"

"It was this or black," she said simply, ignoring his loaded question.

"I definitely like red better. That dress looked damn good on you, too. I'll enjoy seeing it again. Although be warned…it does things to me."

His voice smoldered, and Lauren lowered her eyes. The man could really turn up the heat when he tried.

He spotted her cow slippers on the floor and picked them up. "Don't forget the real reason we came."

"I won't," Lauren said. She took the slippers from

him and placed them in a side flap of the garment bag. "All I need is my makeup and then we can go."

She stepped into the bathroom and retrieved her makeup case. Within moments, she'd zipped up her bag and Justin had lifted it over his shoulder.

"So what should we do tonight?" he asked.

"Do?" They were in the living room, and Lauren stopped so abruptly that he almost ran into the back of her.

He shifted the garment bag to his other shoulder. "Yeah, do. You're feeling better. How about we order some bland carryout that won't upset your stomach and rent a movie or something?"

It sounded like a date. She stared at him, trying to assess his motives. Was this just another attempt to butter her up, to get her to "date" him?

"Don't you have your poker game tonight?" she asked.

"Nah. We canceled and declared a hiatus until after New Year's. So I'm all yours."

Oh, to have him truly all hers. That might really be something. But he wasn't. Maybe she should just tell him what she'd overheard. Maybe she should clear the air as he'd said, instead of letting her feelings fester. No. She wanted to talk to Jeff first.

"Justin, you don't have to stay in because of me. Really, if you have something better to do, go do it. I'm fine." She went over to the bookshelf and pulled out the first book her fingers touched. "I can always read."

His eyebrow arched. "You're going to read *Hamlet* or *King Lear* just for fun?"

She'd retrieved a volume of the complete tragedies of William Shakespeare, a textbook she'd had to purchase in college and never resold at the end of the course.

She gave a short laugh. "Sure, why not? You know how they always do Shakespeare in Forest Park each summer. This year it's supposed to be a tragedy. And I like *Hamlet*."

"Ah. I see. You like guys who have a thing for their mothers. Okay, then," he said, his teasing obvious. "I now know what I need to do."

He turned serious again and made a motion toward the front door. "Come on, let's go. And no, to answer your earlier question. I don't have anything else to do tonight. I'm not the jet-setting playboy you think I am. I'm often home. I happen to like it there."

"It's a nice house," she said. "Especially since it's decorated so well."

He grinned. "Exactly. So let's get back to it. I'm hungry. How does pasta sound? Will a white sauce be okay or do you still have to avoid milk products?"

"I'm sure I can eat those now. They say you should avoid them only if your stomach is unsettled. I'm beyond that stage, which of course means that your shoes are safe."

"My shoes thank you but really didn't mind. Pasta it is."

They exited her condo and within minutes were in his car. Justin used his cell phone and dialed the restaurant, and they stopped and picked up dinner on the way home.

Home. Lauren blinked as the garage door closed behind Justin's car. She didn't live there. This was not her home. But before she could contemplate why she'd thought of his place as home, Justin had ushered her inside.

While they ate, they discovered that both of them were movie buffs, although of different genres. Justin liked action and adventure films, while Lauren preferred classic romantic comedies.

After they'd finished dinner, Lauren vetoed all Justin's DVD movie choices and voted against playing Scrabble. Instead, they settled on a game of Trivial Pursuit. Except for her occasional coughing, which the doctor had said would take a few weeks to clear up, Lauren found herself enjoying the evening. She rolled the die and clapped her hands when the number five appeared.

"Finally. Okay, I'm going to try again. Pink—" Lauren slid her piece the five spaces "—for a pie."

They were sitting on pillows on the floor, around the square coffee table, having moved the nutcracker statues Justin had bought the day before. Lauren was sitting directly on Justin's left, and she watched him expectantly.

Justin pulled the blue-edged Trivial Pursuit card from the holder, keeping the answers on the back covered with his hand. "Okay, pink pie. Boy, this is so easy."

"It better be. It's not fair that you got all the easy questions earlier."

He raised and lowered his eyebrows Groucho Marx style. "It's luck, baby. Luck."

Lauren laughed. She'd been having a great time tonight, except for the fact that she was losing the game. "Yeah, right. That sports question on who won the 1964 Olympic boxing medal was difficult."

"It was the light-heavyweight gold medal," Justin teased. "Remember? Cassius Clay?"

"Well, I certainly won't forget it now," Lauren retorted. "It cost me. I've only got two pies and you've got four."

"You should get your pink pie here," Justin replied. "Ready?" He paused, laughing at the look she gave him. "You'll know this. The cover of the Rolling Stones' *Sticky Fingers* album cover has what?"

"A zipper!" Lauren grabbed for the game-piece bag before Justin even told her that she was correct.

"See," Justin teased. "You at least know rock 'n' roll. Do you have K–SHE on your radio dial?"

"No. But it's only one scan past the country station. My radio stops at it every time."

Justin coughed his disappointment. "Bad girl. I guess your only redeeming feature is that you like the Rolling Stones."

She feigned indignation. "I hope I do. I saw them in concert the last time they came through. What? Don't believe that a simple girl like me could like the Stones?

I bet you had me pegged as a totally alternative chick, didn't you?"

She looked like an exuberant child and her delight at the small victory at his expense made her face glow. Justin decided he liked it a lot.

He gave a huge sigh. "I'm not going to comment on how I had you pegged, because it could ruin my reputation of giving you grief. Anyway, you're making a comeback."

He sipped his beer as he studied her. *Well, Jeff, you're the one who put me up to this.* Not that Justin found himself minding. He loved the original Trivial Pursuit game as much as the Samoa-brand Girl Scout cookies.

Unfortunately, he was only able to indulge in both of them the same amount—once a year. And Lauren was a worthy opponent. She knew a lot of trivial facts, which made him proud. Lauren was brains and beauty. His twin brother was the big idiot.

Justin watched as Lauren attempted to maneuver the pink pie piece into her round blue holder. Instead, it tumbled out of her fingers and onto the floor. As she bent over to search for it, Justin took the moment to stare unabashedly, then covered his actions by looking at the Christmas tree when she faced him once more.

She was driving him crazy. He wanted Lauren Brown. Even more, he wanted to see her happy. She deserved to be happy.

Lauren popped the elusive piece in and picked up the die. She rolled and moved her game piece. "Orange."

Justin reached for another card. "'What pro sport did Wilt Chamberlain play after basketball?'" Justin asked, peeking at the answer.

"Um…baseball." Lauren's forehead creased as she guessed. She waited hopefully, as if willing him to cheat and tell her she was right.

"No!" Justin handed her the card triumphantly. "Volleyball. You were thinking of Michael Jordan."

Lauren double-checked the answer as Justin grabbed the die. She stood up suddenly and reached for her glass. "Hey," Justin protested. "My house. You're the patient. I'll get it for you. Sit down."

"I'm fine, Justin. I'd like more orange juice and I can get it myself. You're making me feel like an invalid, which I am not." She lifted up her cup. "By the way, don't peek at those cards while I'm gone. And I'm not daring you, either. Just don't peek."

Justin chuckled. How appropriate. "Don't you trust me?" he called after her. He heard the refrigerator open before she called back, "No."

He waited until she was in the room. The die came to a stop and he announced, "I'm on the orange pie."

"I don't believe it." Lauren took a long drink of her orange juice before settling back down and reaching for a card. "You're killing me. I thought this would at least be a fair match."

Her face crumpled as she read the question. "I don't believe this." She shot him a mock-evil look. "You did cheat. You rearranged these cards, didn't you?"

He held up his hands in a surrender gesture. "On my honor, no."

"I don't believe you. Okay. 'What's the highest hand in straight poker?'"

"A royal flush," Justin said victoriously. "Hand me that bag, will you?" He gestured toward the bag of pie pieces.

"Ooh." Lauren pouted and reached for her juice. "You're just too lucky."

"Yeah, I am," Justin said. But he wasn't talking about the game. He was referring to her company. Her brown eyes darkened, and she took a sip of juice so that she had an excuse to look away.

The movement of her lips was so simple, yet so seductive without trying to be. He bit his bottom lip and waited for Lauren to hand him the bag. Perhaps some conversation might help.

"Did you know that the odds are sixty-four thousand to one of ever getting a royal flush? In all my days of playing poker, I've never seen one. And, yes, I'm pretty lucky every Friday night, come to think of it."

Okay, that had sounded inane. He also hadn't gotten his pie piece. "All right, I don't think I'm lucky enough here to get my pie piece."

He reached over her lap to get the bag. Lauren tossed it over his head.

"I'm being a spoilsport." She grinned like the Cheshire cat as he leaned over to retrieve the bag.

Justin fished out an orange piece and wedged it in his pie container. "Ah, me agrees that you're a spoilsport."

Not really angry and more just playful, she glared at him. "Roll, cheater."

Justin took the die and rolled. "Brown."

Lauren grabbed another card and pretended to cry. "Now I know that you switched the cards. This cannot be happening to me." She reached for her juice, deliberately delaying the reading of the question. "You know, I was never an unlucky person until I met you."

"You got lucky when you met me."

"Ha. By whose definition? I work with you—I get sick, literally. I toss my cookies on your shoes and end up at your place, where I eat lots of soup and lose at Trivial Pursuit."

"Stop digressing and read," he prodded.

"Fine. Here's your question. 'What are the first three words in the Bible?'"

"In the beginning." Justin grabbed the die. "I honestly didn't know this game had such easy questions in it. Come on, number one."

Lauren sipped her juice and watched as the one appeared. Justin grinned innocently. "Yellow pie."

She drew the card from the box and skimmed the question. "You win," she said.

He won? How? "I'm not trying to torment you, but you have to ask me the question first, Lauren."

He sipped his beer and looked at her over the rim of the bottle. He had gotten a series of easy questions, and he admired how good a sport she'd really been. From the way they rubbed each other wrong in the office, this game had had the potential to be ugly. Instead, it had been fun, and they'd found themselves actually teasing each other.

"Remember, you wanted to play this game. I voted for Scrabble."

"Rub it in, just rub it in," Lauren responded as she turned the card over. "I can be a good sport. I can avoid killing the inventor of this game or its winner. Oh, that's you. So, 'What age followed the Bronze Age?'"

"The Iron Age." Justin grabbed a yellow piece to fill his pie.

Lauren put the card back in the box. "Okay, we're done."

"Don't I need to go up the middle?" he asked.

"That's okay," Lauren replied, shaking her head. The lights of the Christmas tree shimmered off her hair, dancing in a hypnotic pattern.

He paused. While it *had* been a fun game, it hadn't been comfortable. He ached in certain places. So, did he really need to finish the game when such a beautiful woman sat beside him?

His fingers itched to thread themselves through her hair. He'd love nothing more than to kiss her. She coughed, and he knew that kissing her was out of the question. Not until she was well. Then…oh, then he would kiss her. There was no doubt in his mind about that. Now that his brother was out of the way…

But not tonight. Tonight wasn't about kissing, it was about proving that they could get along and that he wanted her, really wanted her for herself.

Justin reached for his bottle and saluted her. His eyes mocked her playfully. "I'll drink to your loss."

"You are a jerk." Lauren set her empty juice glass on the table. Then she did the truly unexpected. She threw her pillow at him. Justin blocked the soft flying square with his left arm, somehow avoiding dropping the bottle that was in his right hand. He set the bottle on the floor, out of the way, scrambled to his knees and lunged for her. Trivial Pursuit pieces went flying as he wrestled her gently to the wooden floor.

His face hovered inches from hers. "You asked for this. You've been asking for this ever since you asked me yesterday if I dared. I may not be able to kiss you, Ms. Lauren Brown, but you can still pay."

"Oh, I'm scared," Lauren said.

She giggled as his fingers touched her skin, tickling every place he could. Lauren wiggled and tried to push him away.

"Stop, no." Lauren laughed. "Please." She laughed some more, the tortured laugh of one who was enjoying every bit of the tickling. Then she started to cough.

Justin let her up immediately and had her sit up. "Are you okay?"

"Fine," she said in between coughs. He cradled her against him.

"I shouldn't have done that. I'm sorry."

"No." Lauren coughed again. "I'm fine."

But she wasn't, and he knew he should have been more sensitive. He placed his left arm around her shoulders. Since her orange juice was empty, he handed her the glass of water he'd gotten for her earlier.

They leaned back against the sofa, and Lauren rested her head on Justin's firm, broad chest. He encircled her in his arms, his left hand absently weaving its way into her hair. She had such soft, silky tresses.

Once again, he wanted to kiss her. He had wanted to kiss those beautiful lips most of the day. Now, with her in his arms…

Just because Jeff was out of the picture didn't mean that Justin stopped being a man of honor. He forced the image of Mother Teresa into his brain so that he could contain himself, tamp down his raging desire. He then made conversation, although, as the words left his lips, he knew he might be treading on even more dangerous territory than kissing her.

"I have a question for you," he said.

"What?" She started to lift her head, but his hand in her hair made her pause and caused her to rest her head against his chest again.

"Okay, this is actually a hard question for me to ask, especially considering how you feel about Jeff. Plus,

I'm worried about sexual harassment and how we act at work and all that, so believe me, that's not it when I ask this."

"You're making no sense. So just ask. What is it?"

He took a deep breath and Lauren's body shifted in rhythm as his chest moved. "Well, I wondered if you would consider being my date tomorrow night."

She seemed surprised, but she didn't lift her head off his chest. Part of him hoped she'd try again, but she didn't. "Your date?" she asked.

"Yes, for the Christmas party. As in you and I go together. I mean, we're going together, but I mean, be together. I would like it if you would accompany me to the Christmas party as my date."

"Oh."

That was the only word she said and he wished he could see her face—by seeing her expression, he might have some idea what she was thinking. He kept himself calm by massaging her neck. "I mean, if it's a bad idea, then forget it."

"No, it's not a bad idea," Lauren replied.

"So you'll go?"

"I didn't say that," she said.

She pulled away slightly and he let her go. She paused and faced him. She had the most beautiful eyes he'd ever seen and they'd been haunting his dreams.

Lauren nodded suddenly. "Why not?" she said. "We'll try it."

She hadn't said no. "Try it?" he echoed.

She nodded again, her honey-colored hair dancing on her shoulders. He tucked some wayward strands behind her ear.

"Yes. I think it might be a good idea. We'll try going somewhere together. Maybe in the long run it'll help us get along better. After all, this week has helped. We're not snapping at each other so much. This game was a lot of fun and proved we could be adversaries without being at war the way we are sometimes in the office."

"Exactly," Justin said as relief filled him. "Although I don't want us to be at war in the office any more than you do. I will promise to work on that."

"So we have a date," Lauren said.

"Yeah, a date," he said.

She frowned suddenly as if remembering something. "And you're sure about tomorrow night?"

His eyes narrowed. Was she changing her mind? "Of course I am. Why?"

"I have to go early and make sure the room is set up right. Although we hired an events coordinator, there are things that only I can do. Like, make sure the personalized champagne flutes are at every table and that they have the gift certificates in them."

Those things. They'd argued about those right before she'd gotten sick on his shoes. That seemed so long ago. "Then I'll help you do whatever needs to be done," Justin said.

"Okay." She lifted herself out of his arms, stood and stretched. His mouth dried at the sight. "I'm tired," she said. "Do you mind if I call it a night?"

"No," he said quickly. He scrambled to his feet. "Absolutely not. I feel guilty that I kept you up this late, anyway."

She glanced at the grandfather clock on the far wall. "It's only eight."

"Time doesn't matter when you have the flu. Come on, didn't you want to read *Hamlet?*"

"Yes," Lauren said, knowing that he was teasing her. "Yes, as a matter of fact I did."

AN HOUR LATER, Lauren pushed the book away. While reading *Hamlet* was better than reading *Romeo and Juliet*—that story of star-crossed lovers seemed a little too real—she hadn't felt much like reading. She was finding herself understanding Hamlet's inner torture. She was understanding Ophelia. Was Lauren herself going mad? She'd agreed to a date with Justin Wright. Her only consolation: at least no prince of the Danes existed in her life.

She blew her nose and tossed the tissue in the trash can. After tucking her into bed and handing her her book, Justin had left and gone out to watch a video. The closed bedroom door muted the sounds of the action-adventure flick she really hadn't wanted to see. Even reading had held more appeal than spending more time with him.

Spending time with him did things to her that she couldn't control. She still couldn't believe she'd caved. She'd agreed to a date with Justin Wright.

She'd planned on saying no. That would have been the best way to thwart his goal of having a relationship with her for at least a week. But when he'd asked with such sincerity, she hadn't had the heart to say no. She'd just have to make him want to dump her long before the week was out if that was all this dating stuff was really about.

Deep down, though, she hoped it wasn't. She wanted a date with Justin Wright. He'd asked her despite what he called her feelings for his brother. Oh, Lauren now knew what those feelings for Jeff really were: her ticking biological clock and her fear of being alone. Jeff Wright had been only Lauren's desire to make something out of nothing, to take what was safe and secure and settle for it instead of true love and happiness. He'd been an easy way out. Thank goodness he'd been wise enough to know it.

And when Lauren had gotten tired of being Jeff's pal, she'd discovered Justin, the man who'd always been under her skin in one way or another.

Justin Wright was not safe and secure. He stirred volatile feelings in her. Passion, anger, joy, disappointment and everything else. He had the power to make her happy, which gave him the power to hurt her, as well.

But that was what life and love were about. Being with him reminded her that she was alive, that she was able to feel.

Her gut instincts told her that he never would hurt her. Told her that Justin Wright treated her too tenderly for that. Her instincts also told her that Justin Wright wanted her. He wanted to kiss her. He wanted to make love to her. He wanted her.

And she wanted him back, despite his words to his brother. She wanted to explore the man who had bought her a Christmas ornament just because he wanted to see her happy.

What she couldn't do yet was believe. But she'd at least risk one date. And somehow she'd have to keep her fragile heart intact in the process.

She was falling in love with Justin Wright.

Chapter Ten

The Wright Solutions Christmas party started at six-thirty, with dinner to be served at seven. Lauren and Justin arrived at three-thirty that afternoon.

"I guess I should have told you we'd need to be here this early when you proposed our date," Lauren said. "I feel a bit guilty. I do have a committee that will help."

"It doesn't matter," Justin said. He lifted the garment bag containing his tux and Lauren's dress from the back of his Cadillac before the valet whisked the car away. "You said we had a hotel room?"

"We don't have a room. Wright Solutions does. It's for changing into our outfits. A few of the social committee volunteers will be early, as well. If they want, they'll store their things in the room until after the party, since the coatroom won't be open yet."

"Oh."

They entered the hotel lobby and Justin followed Lauren to the front desk.

"It's a small price to pay for having a perfect banquet hall and a clean dress. Trust me, never change in a public bathroom in a hotel. It's way too awkward. Just factor the room into the cost of the event, if necessary."

Lauren set her briefcase on the counter and opened it. She retrieved some papers that rested right on top.

"No wonder this party cost a small fortune," Justin remarked.

"Put your mind at ease. I got the hotel to toss in the room free when I booked the ballroom, Mr. Frugal." She smiled at the front-desk clerk and passed him a copy of the reservation. "Lauren Brown of Wright Solutions."

"My brother calls me Mr. Frugal. I hate it. Just because I hunt for bargains and refuse to pay full price unless I have to does not make me worthy of being called a name."

"Sorry," Lauren said. She looked at him, and Justin could tell she meant her apology. "You're right and I won't call you that anymore. It was rude of me and I should know better."

The desk clerk coughed discreetly. "Ms. Brown, everything is taken care of. Your credit card is already on file for incidentals. Would you like one or two keys?"

"Two," Lauren said. She turned back to Justin.

"And besides," he went on, "although I don't like being called Mr. Frugal, being frugal is a good thing. It's what allowed this company to expand and make it through some of the lean times, especially some of the dot-com disasters. My role has always been that of the corporate conscience."

"Well, now that the company is a bit flush, it's time to reward all those employees for being there for you, just as Jared suggested. Like I've said, a Christmas party outside the office with something besides beer and nachos creates goodwill that will go a long, long way. So lighten up. Just about everyone is coming. It's going to be a blast."

She'd totally misunderstood him and taken his words personally. That was not how he'd meant them, and not how he wanted to start their date. "I never said this wouldn't be a success. All the work I've seen you do has been top-notch. My only regret is that Jared won't be here. This company really is his baby."

The desk clerk handed Lauren two electronic passkeys. "You're on the tenth floor. Room 1061. Up the elevators and to the right. Enjoy your stay."

"Thanks." Lauren grabbed her briefcase and began walking toward the elevators. "He can be here next year. A man only gets married once. Well, hopefully." She paused as a coughing fit consumed her.

Justin was instantly worried. He shifted the garment bag and spun her gently around to face him. "Are you okay?"

"Fine," Lauren managed to say as the coughing subsided. She pressed the elevator button. "I'm much better now that the fever's gone and I've gotten rid of the runny nose. I'm getting tired of this cough, that's for sure. I'm due for my cough medicine. I'll take it when we get upstairs."

They rode the elevator to the tenth floor and found the room. It was a basic hotel room with a king-size bed, desk, chair and television—really nothing fancy. Lauren tossed her briefcase on the bed. "Just hang the garment bag in the closet or lay it on the bed and we'll go downstairs. I want to see the ballroom."

Leaving so quickly seemed like a waste of a perfectly good bed and hotel room to Justin, but he could tell Lauren was all business right now. Already she was halfway out the door and leaving him behind. "Come on," she called from the hall.

Two hours of work later, the ballroom met Lauren's expectations. Justin had spent most of his time moving things and carrying boxes full of Wright Solution presents. He'd also set out more champagne flutes than he could count. He hadn't worked like this since he'd waited tables during college.

"I'm impressed," he told Lauren as he watched her tweak the last decoration. "I didn't realize how much effort goes into one of these parties."

"A lot," Lauren admitted. "Even with hiring the party planner and her staff, there are always things left to do. When you're in charge, you always should be on-site, especially at an event this big."

"Well, let's go upstairs and get ready. Or I, at least, need to get ready. I want a shower. Some of those cardboard boxes were really dirty."

"See, I told you, a room is—"

"Yeah, yeah," Justin said, cutting her off. He grinned at his defeat but refused to truly concede. "Just remember that I whipped you in Trivial Pursuit."

"Oh, so we're even now." Lauren rewarded him with a knowing expression as she followed him from the ballroom.

"Yeah," Justin said, making his smile even cheekier so that he could incite another reaction, any reaction, from her. "For now. That sounds good. Let's go prepare for our date, shall we?"

All she did was smile, but it was enough.

LAUREN TAPPED her foot on the carpet impatiently. Justin Wright was about to make her late.

"Are you almost done?" she called. She had no idea a man could take so long in the bathroom.

Okay, so he'd been in there maybe fifteen minutes, tops. She'd needed a lot more time to freshen up. But the first of the guests would be arriving in ten minutes and it was important that someone from Corporate be downstairs to greet them.

Lauren paced, her sparkly red shoes, à la Dorothy in *The Wizard of Oz*, peeking out from underneath her floor-length gown. She raised her fist to bang on the bathroom door, almost hitting Justin square in the chest when the door opened.

"Sorry," she mumbled, her face flushing. "Uh, uh…"

Oh, dear Lord. He wore nothing but a towel slung low around his waist. Her throat constricted; her mouth dried. A few water droplets still clung to his smooth, muscular chest, one of them daring to snake its way downward to…. Lauren dropped her gaze to her feet, which proved to also be a mistake, as his bare knees and toes were clearly visible to her and equally as tantalizing.

"I had to shave," he said. "Five o'clock shadow and stuff. Just let me grab my clothes and I'll be ready in a minute."

He smelled wonderful, that divine combination of clean male skin and aftershave. Lauren swallowed. Perhaps having a room wasn't a good idea. "How about I wait in the hall while you change. Bathroom steam and all that. Getting into my clothes was pretty miserable and…"

She was babbling like an idiot, but she couldn't help it. If she even thought of what was underneath that towel…oh my.

"I'm sure you could just turn your back, right? After all, we are both adults."

He knew, the cad. He knew what heat was tracking its way through her. He knew she was affected. The collision course that they were on was perfectly clear. She couldn't play the game. Despite his sins, despite his flaws and his words to Jeff, she couldn't make Justin

Wright want and groan—she couldn't make him pay—without her being in the exact same state. The lingerie she wore moved slightly, reminding Lauren of exactly what had transpired the last time she'd worn it. Lauren had to escape.

"There's that small seating area by the elevators. I'll meet you there. Five minutes or I leave you behind and go downstairs without you."

He grinned. "Even though this is our date, how about I meet you downstairs, Lauren? I don't want you stressed, and I know you. You have to make sure everything is in place. Go on. I'm a big boy, and I can make my entrance by myself. Who knows, maybe you'll miss me. Just remember, once this party gets going, tonight is not about work."

He let the rest go unsaid and Lauren simply stammered an "Uh," before her thoughts jumbled. She nodded and fled the room.

When she reached the ballroom, her trained eye instantly noticed that everything was in place. She paused to inhale a deep breath and relax. The social committee volunteers manned the greeting table. The hotel staff had opened the coatroom. The bartenders waited. A few early birds had already trickled in, finding places and finding friends.

Everything was perfect.

"Hi, Lauren. Great job. I think we're ready," a female voice said.

Lauren turned to see Tori, one of the tech-support crew and a social committee member. "We are," Lauren said. "Thanks for all your help tonight."

"Not a problem. Now that I'm officially off duty, I'm going to get a very large cocktail. I haven't had one in a while, and it sounds especially good after rebuilding Cybertech's servers all day yesterday."

"You were in Chicago with Jeff?"

"Yes. It took five of us to get the job done so that we could make it back here in time. He's great to work for, though. I couldn't imagine anyone better." Tori paused as if she'd said too much. "Anyway, I'll catch you later. Have fun tonight." Tori moved off toward the bar.

"So, tell me, are you having fun?" Justin's voice tickled in her ear and Lauren jumped. He placed a reassuring hand on her arm, and her arm tingled under his magical touch. "Sorry. I didn't mean to scare you."

"I didn't hear you come up," she said.

"Obviously." He slid his hand to cup her elbow, trailing a fiery path on her skin. "Let's go find our table. We're not assigned one, are we?"

"Actually, yes. There's one reserved at the very front by the podium. Not a head table—you vetoed that—but one that blends in with the rest."

"Ah, but with a better view."

"You are speaking," she said as they wove their way through the round tables.

"Only to welcome everyone," he said. "The rest of the program is all yours and the committee's."

They reached the reserved table and Lauren inwardly sighed with satisfaction. Holiday china rested on pure white table linens. Floral arrangements with lit candles inside hurricane glasses centered each table, and red-and-green-colored ribbons extended from the arrangements to envelopes containing holiday cards and raffle tickets. The champagne flutes held the little gift certificate scrolls.

Instead of a band, the committee had opted for a disc jockey, and warm, classic holiday tunes flowed from the speakers. Justin held out her chair. "Who will be at the table with us?" he asked.

"It's open seating for the most part," Lauren said. "I know Jeff's planning to sit with us, and Clint, but really, they're the only ones I know of."

But their table of eight soon filled up with Jeff, one of his single male co-workers who was also going stag, another couple and Clint, who had brought Hilary, the woman Lauren had met at the chamber dinner.

Justin gave his welcome speech, dinner began, and after a delicious meal of filet mignon and chicken piccata, followed by cherry-topped cheesecake for dessert, Lauren stood to go begin announcing the winners of the raffle.

The committee had worked hard on prizes, and oohs and aahs were heard as people discovered they'd won spa gift certificates, free movie rentals, a weekend at the lake and other goodies such as one extra vacation day.

"We will start the secret-Santa exchange in exactly forty minutes," Lauren announced, "so make sure if you haven't done so already that you who are participating put your gift on the tables over by the back wall. And now, our own vice president of Public Relations and Marketing, Clint Seaver, is going to lead us in the first dance. Please feel free to join him."

The deejay started playing "In the Mood," and pretty soon the dance floor was crowded. Lauren came back over to the table and surveyed the crowd. Success.

"Are you planning on sitting back down?" Justin asked.

"Not yet," she said. She looked over Justin's head to the back wall. People were placing their gifts on the table and already peeking to see if they could find the gift tag that bore their name. Everything was perfect, but then again, something wasn't right. As if she'd forgotten to do something important, but for the life of her she had no idea what.

"Then would you like to dance?" Justin asked.

She had to figure out what she'd forgotten to do. "I have to make sure…"

Justin pushed his chair out and stood. His six-foot body topped hers and a thrill raced through her. "This isn't about work, Lauren. Now, take my hand and follow me."

She opened her mouth as if to challenge him, but

something in the steel of his green eyes made her pause. She knew better than to dare him. His outstretched hand engulfed hers as she took it, and within moments she was on the dance floor.

He felt divine. Whatever she'd forgotten suddenly didn't matter. She was lost in Justin's arms, which was right where she belonged and needed to be.

The music changed, but still he held her. As they danced to their third song, the moment was not lost on Jeff. He waited only until Clint returned to the table and Hilary had excused herself to the ladies' room.

"I think we've got success," Jeff said.

"Sure about that?" Clint said.

"Yeah. I am. I got into it with him the other day. While you were starting the dance, he told me that tonight is a date. A real date, and not just to spite me, either, even though he spent at least two minutes warning me to stay away from her tonight. Look at him. I've never seen him like this. He's definitely in love with her."

"I'll be…" Clint narrowed his gaze and studied Justin and Lauren. "Maybe the flu did what we couldn't."

"Perhaps," Jeff said. "But until I see them wed, I'm not going to be satisfied. Not even one bit. I'll do whatever it takes."

Lauren and Justin danced one more song before Lauren pulled herself out of Justin's arms and left to check on the secret-Santa exchange. Everything was perfect here, too.

The PR department secretary was in charge, and she was next to the table. "It's under control, Lauren," Trisha said. "They're all here—or at least, it looks like it. Sue checked them off. Anyway, I've got an extra or two stashed underneath the table just in case. We're ready when you are."

Lauren glanced at the thin gold watch on her wrist. "Ten minutes," she said. She went over to the bar and requested another soft drink. Still taking her medication and still feeling a bit weak, she wasn't up for anything alcoholic.

She turned around, and almost ran into Jeff. Her glass wobbled, and he steadied it.

"Hey," he said. He held up his bottle of beer so that the bartender knew to get him another. "How are you?"

"Better," Lauren said.

"So Justin is giving you plenty of tender loving care?"

"Actually, I want to talk to you about that. I've got to do the secret Santa, but afterward, can you give me a few minutes of your time?"

Jeff reached for the new bottle of beer. "Of course I can. Is everything okay? My brother is treating you all right, isn't he?"

He was sweet to be concerned. "Yes, but I have a few questions for you. I really need them answered. Please."

Jeff shrugged and took a sip. "Not a problem. I'm happy to help. But be assured that he's a good guy, Lauren. And if he isn't, I'll take care of him for you. I can still beat him up, you know." He grinned at his joke.

"Let's talk right after secret Santa, maybe during a dance or something. I've got to go make the announcement getting it started," she said.

Carrying her soda, she made her way back to the podium. The music stopped, and she began. "Ladies and gentlemen, for those of you participating in the secret-Santa exchange, it's time to meet me back at the table. The way it works is simple. Just find your present and be sure to thank the giver!"

As Lauren returned to the tables, the music started again, this time just a notch lower in volume and waltzier than earlier.

All around her she heard the squeals of women who were delighted with their gifts. She glanced at the gift table, where only a few presents remained. She frowned. Once again she had the feeling that something wasn't right.

Trisha came up to her. "Lauren, I didn't see your gift."

"Oh, my!" Lauren's hand flew to her face. That was it! How could she have forgotten? Even seeing the table tonight hadn't jogged her memory. Having the flu and staying at Justin's had really gotten her out of sync. "Trisha, my envelope! It's upstairs in my briefcase! I didn't even open it. What will I do? Wait—you said you had extra gifts."

Trisha nodded. "I do. I'll get one out from under the table. Oh, here he comes. Sorry. Be prepared. You have each other and he's going to hand you his gift himself.

I'll hurry." Trisha mouthed the word *Sorry* again and stepped back.

"I'm your secret Santa," a familiar voice said.

Lauren turned. Oh, no. She'd forgotten all about her envelope—and she'd had Justin. She who loved Christmas and all the secret-Santa events. She who had cornered Justin into decorating his house. She'd forgotten.

Then again, it was Justin. He'd taken her in, nursed her to health. She should have bought him something personal. Not just the generic something that Trisha was providing. There was no way she could hand him one of those gifts. Guilt plagued Lauren. "Hi," she said.

"Hi," Justin replied. He held out a small wrapped package, even smaller than the one the ornament he'd given her had come in. The gold bow on the thin three-inch rectangular box sparkled. "Merry Christmas, Lauren. This is for you."

"Thank you." Lauren accepted the present but didn't unwrap it. Her hand trembled and she took a deep breath. She'd blown it, big-time. "I have a confession. I didn't open my envelope. It's still in my briefcase upstairs. I forgot all about it. I'm so sorry. I didn't get you anything."

He looked neither surprised nor disappointed. "You've had the flu," Justin said. "You have every excuse in the book not to remember everything. Just be happy with what I got you and that will be enough for me."

He saw her torn expression and put a finger under her

chin, lifted her chin and gazed into her eyes. "Seriously. I really had fun picking it out. It caught my eye when I was out buying decorations, and the moment I saw it, I knew it was you. Now, open the box."

He stepped back to give her space and Lauren undid the bow. As she slid her finger under the paper, the events of the ballroom disappeared into the background. All she saw was the red box, the white tissue and, beneath it, the fragile puffed heart pendant. Woven fourteen-carat gold trimmed the heart, and painted pansies so purple they were almost red decorated the painted white surface. The metal pendant hung on a gold chain that Lauren instantly knew was also real. Justin had given her something fifteen times more expensive than the twenty-dollar limit the committee had imposed.

"This is beautiful," she finally managed to say.

Relief crossed his face. "I'm glad you like it. It's you. Soft. Beautiful. Dainty, yet strong."

His words touched her, and a small cry escaped her. "I can't accept this."

"Why not?" He frowned and Lauren realized she'd upset him. Couldn't he see what this meant?

Someone appeared as a shadow to Lauren's right, but Lauren waved the person away. "Justin, this cost a fortune. What does this mean? Is this some sort of game to you? What do you want from me?"

"I—" Justin began

The person to Lauren's right moved closer and Lauren turned. "It's okay, Trisha. I told…"

But it wasn't Trisha who stood next to her. Jeff did, and he didn't look as though he understood that he'd interrupted something.

"Hey, guys, what's up?" His gaze went over her head as he scanned the crowd as if searching for someone. "Lauren, if we're going to do that dance and talk, let's go do it now. I'm planning to cut out of here early."

Lauren opened her mouth to tell Jeff it wasn't a good time, but already Justin had taken a step back. "Go," Justin said, his anger at the interruption evident in his tone. She clutched the present in her hand as Jeff led her away.

"What's his problem?" Jeff asked as they hit the dance floor. "Don't even tell me he's giving you grief. Not on tonight of all nights. This party is perfect."

"No, he's not," Lauren said. "In fact, he just gave me a lovely secret-Santa gift. But I don't think I can accept it. And that's what I need to talk to you about. I overheard your conversation at his house—"

So fast did Jeff suddenly stop that Lauren almost tripped over his feet. "There she is."

He glanced down at Lauren and she could tell his interest in dancing with her had vanished.

"I know this is important to you, but we've got to continue this later, Lauren. Right now I've got to settle a score. Forgive me, okay? We'll talk soon, I promise."

"Sure," Lauren said. She watched as Jeff walked off.

He went over to a woman. When the woman turned in surprise, Lauren recognized her as Tori, from tech support. Then Jeff cupped Tori's elbow, and although Tori didn't appear too happy about it, they left the ballroom together.

"Lauren, oh, thank goodness." Mae, one of the social committee volunteers who'd arrived early, came up. "I've been looking all over for you. I need to get my stuff out of the hotel room. Can you walk me up? My husband's already outside warming up the car. He's not one to trust valets, especially after an accident in Florida one year."

"No problem," Lauren said, wondering what was happening between Jeff and Tori. "Let's go on up."

HE'D ONLY TURNED AROUND for a moment to get a glass of club soda from the bar. But a moment was all it took, obviously, for him to lose sight of both Lauren and Jeff. Neither was anywhere to be found on the dance floor, and a walk through the ballroom showed that neither was there, either.

He frowned. Maybe he'd been an idiot buying Lauren that necklace. He hadn't meant it as an attempt to win her affection. But he wanted her to see him, finally see him, as something other than Mr. Perfect's imperfect twin.

Heck, when it came right down to it, he was probably more perfect for Lauren than Jeff was. If nothing else, she was perfect for him.

He'd realized that this week. He'd seen her looking like death and he'd still found her beautiful. She intrigued him, and after almost a week in his house, he was certain she'd never bore him. He dreaded her going. He dreaded her telling him that Jeff was the man for her, and that no matter how wonderful he, Justin, was, he wasn't good enough.

His gift wasn't about winning her from his idiot brother. It wasn't about showing his idiot brother that he could make Lauren fall for him. It wasn't revenge for Betty or Boopsie or whatever that girl's name had been their freshman year of college.

No, when he'd purchased that pendant it had been all about Lauren. He wanted a relationship with her. Who could say where it would go? Who could say how long it would last? Whatever it was and would be, he wanted to explore it.

He desired Lauren more than any other female he'd ever known. And the funny thing was, in the back of his mind the term *forever* lingered and suddenly didn't sound scary at all.

But would she want him? Would she be able to view him as anything other than his brother's twin?

As for a first date, this evening wasn't turning out very well. He spotted Clint. Clint and Jeff were tight; maybe he'd know where Jeff and Lauren had gone.

"Hey, Clint," he said as he joined his friend and Hilary at their table. "Having a good time?"

"Yeah, pretty good, I have to admit," Clint said. "So, are you planning on conceding that Lauren was right in hosting this shindig?"

"I've already eaten all the crow possible," Justin said. "However, I'm sure she'll dish up more for me at some point. Speaking of Lauren, we got separated and I think we're now playing tag. Do you know where she went?"

Clint shook his head. "No. Last I saw her was when she and Jeff were dancing. But then next time I glanced over, both of them were off the dance floor. Did you see them, Hilary?"

Hilary shook her head.

"I did," a voice said.

Justin turned. He didn't recognize the woman who'd entered into the conversation. "This is Maggie, Cecil's wife," Clint said.

"I don't know Lauren, but I do know Jeff," the woman said. "He left with a pretty blonde, and the last I saw them, they were headed toward the hotel elevator."

Justin's gut clenched. "Thanks. They had some things to talk about. I'll catch them up there."

"Nice to see you again," Hilary said.

Justin's long stride carried him easily to the ball-room doors. Had Jeff and Lauren gone upstairs? Had his brother all of a sudden realized that Lauren was a desirable woman?

Perhaps Jeff had interrupted Justin's earlier warning to stay away as a challenge. And Lauren was so beautiful tonight. If Jeff had decided to go for it, Justin doubted Lauren could resist. After all, wasn't Jeff her ultimate man, her ultimate fantasy? Wasn't Jeff the man she really wanted?

Jealousy consumed Justin. He had to know. If he didn't stand a chance with the most fascinating woman in his world, better he learn the bitter truth now before things went any further.

Maybe that was why she'd told him she couldn't accept his gift.

"Justin! There you are. I have your secret-Santa gift." Trisha held out an envelope.

He waved her off. "It's okay. Lauren told me that she had me and forgot."

"Oh." Trisha appeared a bit confused. "I had extras in case. I—"

"It's fine." He took the envelope from her. "Sorry, I'm in a hurry. I'm trying to find Lauren."

"Oh. She went upstairs."

"Thanks." Justin walked out into the brightly lit hotel corridor. His tuxedo shirt itched and he ran a finger under his collar as he strode to the elevators. Lauren had gone upstairs.

By the time he'd reached the tenth floor he was in an unfamiliar state. What would he find? Would they be together? Would it be innocent, or would she have shed that dress?

Every time she wore that dress he wanted to get underneath it. His breath sounded ragged even to his ears. He stepped outside the hotel room. He'd never done this before. Did one knock? Or did one just open the door and burst in?

He reached inside his jacket pocket for his passkey and pulled it out, the white plastic ominous in his hand.

He slid it into the door and the light turned green. *In for a penny, in for a pound,* Justin thought as he yanked the handle and pushed the door open.

Chapter Eleven

Lauren realized the door was opening a minute too late. After she'd let Mae out of the room, she had discovered a run in her panty hose. Luckily, she'd packed another pair, and she'd hiked her dress up and had one leg perched on the bed, the other rooted to the floor, when the door fully opened.

There was no time to cover herself.

She'd never seen Justin looking so…she wasn't sure what word to use to describe him. A cross between anger and relief. But there was also something about his expression that she'd never seen before.

Lauren said nothing as Justin poked his head into the bathroom, even into the hall closet. "Where is he?" he finally asked.

She had no clue to whom he was referring. "Do you mean she? Mae just left. She needed her coat. Her husband was warming up the car."

"No, I meant Jeff. People in the ballroom saw you leave with him."

Lauren's fingers stilled on the top of her hose. She only had them up to midthigh. Who knew what Justin could see. "That's impossible. He couldn't be with me when he left with Tori."

He looked confused. "Tori? From tech support?"

"Yes."

"Then why are you undressing?"

He thought that she…oh, my! He actually thought she'd left with Jeff and brought him up here to… Lauren flushed. Justin's lack of trust astounded and angered her on multiple levels.

"For your information, Mr. Caveman—not that I owe you an explanation, but I'll give you one just so your Neanderthal brain can be placated—I am changing my panty hose. The other pair have a huge run in the right calf. They're on the chair over there if you'd like to check for yourself."

She yanked up her hose all the way and put her leg back down, the red dress fluttering to the floor. Then she slipped on her red shoes. Justin began to take a step forward before he stopped the movement and shoved his hands in his pants pockets.

"Sorry," he mumbled.

"You really believe I'd come on a date with you and run off with your brother?" Lauren demanded

His cheek muscle twitched and he didn't answer.

Anger seeped through every pore. "I can see from your expression that you do. You should know I'm not like that. I said I was here with you."

He remained disbelieving. "Or are you just using me to get to Jeff…make him jealous?"

She sputtered as the blow hit. "You're the one sounding jealous."

"Why shouldn't I be jealous? I'm jealous as hell. Just where do I stand? You're the one in love with my brother."

"I am not," Lauren retorted without thinking, without even registering that Justin had just admitted his jealousy.

"Really. Your precious heart changed overnight? Poof, in love. Poof, out."

She stomped her foot, the red shoe having no impact on the carpet. "I don't believe you just said that! You make me sound like a tramp! As if your motivations give you any room to talk. You have no right to sit as judge and jury over my behavior. I know exactly why you asked me out tonight."

"What—because I want to be with you? Hell, Lauren, I'm not going to stand here and argue with you. What else do you want me to do? Beg? I'm not going to beg."

He turned suddenly and walked to the door.

Then, just as quickly, he turned back. "I feel like Rhett Butler demanding Scarlett get that other guy out of her head. Damn it, I am not going to just walk away from you. Not this time. I'm sick of chivalry. It can go to hell. I'm going to do what I should have done in the first place. I'm going to kiss him right out of your head."

"What?" Lauren's eyes widened as Justin walked back toward her. The intensity in his gaze would have perhaps frightened any other woman, but Lauren was not any other woman. She was Justin's equal. She also instinctively knew he would never hurt her, and her gut instincts were never wrong.

She had been seducing the right man that night.

"You're a movie buff, too," Justin said, his voice low. "I'm sure you know the scene where Rhett Butler says Scarlett needs lots of kissing."

"I do. So, are you planning to be Rhett Butler?" She'd meant for the words to sound brave, defiant, almost a dare. Instead, they came out as awe.

"If that's what it takes. You need lots of kissing," Justin said, the tension between them not ebbing, only changing, as both realized that it was finally time. "My kissing."

"Oh, yes," Lauren said.

He touched her cheek gently, his caress fraught with promise. Then he surprised her. "Kiss me," he said. "I'd like it if you kissed me."

She'd kissed him before, but now she was choosing to kiss him, choosing to share and risk a little piece of her soul, if not the whole thing.

She opened to him, feeling the butterfly kisses he bestowed that flitted and flirted until he couldn't resist any longer. Then his mouth took hers completely.

The intense sensations his deep kisses evoked weakened her knees, and she clung to him.

Oh, yes. This was the right man—this was the man time had made her for. Her brain registered that just before it turned its logic off, leaving her body and heart free to feel unimpeded.

And feel she did. Justin's tongue mated with hers and tasted every treasure hidden in her depths. She opened for him like a blossoming flower. Their kisses built anticipation of more passion to come.

His fingers slid underneath her dress strap. She tilted her head to give him further access to her skin and Justin's powerful fingers traveled lower, tracing her collarbones, teasing the hollow between her breasts.

He was her man, she his woman, and both of them knew it. Tonight there would be no interruptions, no stopping the joining that needed to occur, no stopping what fate had ordained.

His tuxedo had to go. Their mouths never parting, she pushed his suit coat off. Removed his tie. Found the buttons of his shirt and undid them one by one. She had him down to his undershirt. With a groan, Justin removed the offending piece of clothing from his body. She had his bare chest under her fingers, and as her fingers found his bare flesh Lauren knew ecstasy.

His chest was toned, strong and finally hers to touch. Skin heated skin as she ran her hands everywhere.

She heard the red zipper as it clicked down; she felt coolness as the dress formed a glittery puddle at her feet. He gasped, and she heard his groan of delight as he discovered the black lingerie that she'd worn just for him.

She moved her hands to the placket of his pants, undid the button and slid the zipper down. He didn't let her go farther, but instead lowered her to the bed, his touch heating her skin.

Her limbs loosened, and she felt as though she were floating on a cloud high above. Never had she felt like this. Justin was now kissing her everywhere, charting new paths. He mapped her body with kisses: tasting, suckling, fondling, and she reveled in it.

His body was made for loving her and he swept her along, everything perfection. He met her every need, bringing her to frenzy after frenzy as he loved every inch of her skin.

When a small rip pierced the night, her eyes flew open. He sensed her withdrawal from him immediately. "What's wrong?" he asked.

"You're prepared," she said. She covered her nakedness with her arms but the gesture was useless. He'd tasted her most intimate secrets; how could she hide from him now?

"I haven't been with anyone in a year," he said, his voice gentle. "I only brought these because I'd hoped, because I wanted…"

He raked a hand through his mussed hair. "I'm botching this up, aren't I? Let me try again. I didn't ask you on this date to seduce you. I didn't give you that necklace to get you into bed. I want you, Lauren Brown, a great deal. I want you so much it hurts. But I want you on your terms, and that's the way it's going to be. There's a cold shower waiting for me if we stop here, but if that's what it takes for me to prove to you that I mean what I say, then that's what it's going to be."

He lay beside her and she stared at him. Since they hadn't turned out the lights, she could study every line, every crease on his face for signs that he was lying.

She saw none.

He was already moving to get out of the bed, and she knew his actions weren't just a ploy to get what he wanted. He meant to give her space, let her decide. He meant every word he'd just said.

"Justin." He was now standing, and he turned, unashamed of the desire that bulged against his undone trousers.

"Kiss me." She lifted her arms and he came back toward her, although not yet into her arms.

"You're sure?" he whispered, his lips against her neck.

"Positive," Lauren said.

For once in her life she was. She and Justin would straighten out the matter of the "bet with Jeff" later, for in her heart she knew from Justin's earlier words that his and Jeff's conversation didn't matter. It wasn't a factor at all.

A smile crossed her face and she boldly reached her hands toward his pants. "I'm absolutely positive. Love me, Justin Wright."

"It will be my pleasure," he said as her hands found him. "My pleasure."

"Oh, no," Lauren said, as touching him simply worked her body back into a frenzy, "it will be my pleasure. All mine."

Justin's lips found hers, and a few moments later, he gave her what she craved, gave her what she needed, as he drove himself into her. He filled her completely, as she'd known he would, made her experience a nirvana that had not existed until him.

As she shattered, she heard his words and knew the real truth.

"Oh, no," he said as he joined her in one last trip over the top. "It's not just your pleasure or mine. It's ours."

MORNING SUN FILTERED through the hotel curtains, causing Lauren to stir. Never had she felt so complete.

Not that she needed a man to complete her.

She'd done fine on her own for twenty-eight years, not counting that one horrific experience with Mike.

Lauren knew that sharing your life was a choice; she also knew that she was still a complete person if she chose not to share hers.

But as she lay next to Justin Wright, sharing her

life with him seemed much more appealing than not sharing it, especially since he would be sharing his in return.

He'd loved her well into the night, loved her in ways Lauren hadn't known would make her feel so wonderful. The memory made her blush. Justin had always concentrated on her needs, her pleasure.

They'd showered together at some point, and afterward he'd placed the heart necklace around her neck. It had been the only thing she'd worn when he'd made love to her again.

There was no doubt in Lauren's mind—they fit together perfectly.

The bedside clock told her it was close to eleven, but Lauren didn't worry about the time. Sometime around six in the morning, when it had become obvious they weren't going to leave bed anytime soon, Justin had arranged late checkout and the delivery of breakfast. Room service had brought up a tray over an hour ago, but she and Justin hadn't touched the continental breakfast, instead opting to make love again. Her stomach growled, but he slept right through that noise.

She smiled. He deserved to rest, she reflected. He'd worked pretty hard at making her happy. She eased out of bed and snagged one of the croissants they'd ordered.

"Eating without me?" Justin was awake, and as he sat up, the sheet fell to expose his naked chest.

"Mmm-hmm," Lauren mumbled through closed lips.

Would he ever stop looking so darn good? She swallowed. "I was hungry and I didn't want to wake you up."

"Don't worry about it. I'm always aware of your movements. Tell me, how are you feeling this morning?"

"Okay. My head hurts just a bit, but I'm overdue for my medicine. Plus, I didn't get much sleep last night."

He grinned sheepishly. "Sorry about that."

"Oh, don't apologize." Lauren opened the small jar of grape jelly and spread some on a croissant. "Believe me when I say that I'm sure I would have protested had I really minded your, ah, attentions."

He grinned and reached for an English muffin. "Actually, I agree with you. If you'd really minded, I'm sure you would have."

She waved the croissant at him. "Hey. What's that supposed to mean?"

He shook his head and winked at her. "You know exactly what I mean. You're one of the most outspoken women I know. In fact, that's one of the things that I like the most about you."

"What? That I have a big mouth?"

He arched his eyebrow. "Oh, yeah. I can think of many things that mouth did last night. Quite well, in fact, if I may give you that compliment. I'm looking forward to the next time that mouth opens on any part of my body."

His sexy talk was causing her desire to flare and Lauren blushed from head to toe. "Okay, I'll concede. You won that round, too."

He gave her a satisfied smile. "I'll make it up to you later."

Lauren reddened even more. "Cad."

"You keep calling me that, so it must be a compliment."

"Bah." She stuck her tongue out at him.

His green eyes darkened. "Ooh, Lauren, I wouldn't do that if I were you. You won't finish that food if you tempt me like that."

As a part of him stirred under the covers, Lauren dared to stick her tongue out again.

"I warned you never to dare me," Justin said. He lunged for her, his English muffin flying onto the floor.

Lauren had just enough time to put her croissant down before he tackled her and rolled her underneath him to kiss her lips.

"Now, that's what I call breakfast," he murmured.

They finally made it to his house about 5:00 p.m. "You do know I'll have to go home at some point," Lauren said as they entered Justin's place.

"Why?" Justin asked. He deposited the garment bag in the laundry room. "Move in with me. I want you here."

Lauren shook her head. "Not yet," she said simply. "Let's see how this relationship goes. I'll stay with you, but I'm not giving up my condo yet or anything like that. I made that mistake once, remember, and I won't do it again."

"You only told me a bit about that."

"I was twenty-two and fresh out of college. Mr. Wonderful, aka Mike, insisted I move in with him and give up my place. I was naive and thought I was in love. So I did. He did a complete Dr. Jekyll and Mr. Hyde. It wasn't pleasant. I'm just glad we never had a joint bank account, as he wanted. I'd like to take this—us—slow."

"I told you, this relationship is on your terms," Justin said. He drew Lauren tightly into his arms. "I mean that, Lauren. I want you to be happy. Every moment that you're with me makes me happy. I don't need more than you can give. I don't want you to ever feel pressured, or that I'm demanding you do things my way. I don't ever want you to think I'm like Mike. And you can believe and trust me when I tell you that I'll always be faithful to you."

"Thank you," Lauren said. His words moved her, and tears came.

"Don't cry, sweetheart. I want what's best for you, even if it's not necessarily what's best for me. There's no rush at all for you to move in permanently. No rush. We have all the time in the world."

Chapter Twelve

By Monday afternoon, Lauren wished she had all the time in the world. With Christmas Eve falling on a Friday, she had only a four-day workweek before Wright Solutions shut down for its all-company holiday between Christmas and New Year. Plus, she'd barely done any of her Christmas shopping. Worse, her mother had called and was making loud noises about going to her sister's in Kansas City for Christmas. Of course Lauren would need to make the trek, as well.

Which brought her to a problem.

Justin hadn't mentioned anything about Christmas. She'd have to talk to him that afternoon. Once they left work, he was taking her to her condo.

"Hey, look who's here. How are you feeling?"

Lauren glanced up. Was it only just a short while ago when she would see Jeff in her office door and her heart would flutter? How silly that crush had been. Jeff had been her buddy and her pal. He was still a friend, but he was also simply Justin's twin. "I'm great," Lauren answered. "How are you?"

"On the fly, as usual. We're upgrading servers over in South County today so I've got to run. But I know you wanted to talk to me and I wanted to let you know I hadn't forgotten. I've got something I want to bounce off you, anyway. I'll be home Wednesday night for sure. You planning to dust your shelves or anything and be around that night?"

She didn't think she and Justin had any plans. "How about we say five and I'll plan to be there."

"Will you be cooking dinner?" Jeff looked hopeful.

"Yes, I can cook dinner, but let me tell you, my days of ironing your shirts are over."

"Can I still bring my laundry over?"

Lauren smiled. "Only because it's Christmas and only if you do it all yourself."

"Great. I'll see you Wednesday night." Jeff saluted her and ducked down the hall.

"So, will I see you at home later?"

Lauren sat forward so fast that her chair thumped her in the back. She'd really have to stop doing that. After more than six months of sitting in her office chair, she'd have thought she'd learned by now. "Hey," she said.

Justin entered her office and closed the door tightly behind him. "Hey, yourself. I take it I startled you."

"You always seem to, especially when I'm deep in

thought. I was just trying to brainstorm what to do with the summer ad campaign. We're doing great on word of mouth, but exposure remains the key. We've got some major trade conferences coming up, and I'd like to have a unifying theme. Thus my state of deep concentration."

While Lauren had been telling him that, Justin had moved behind her to snake his fingers through her hair. "Ah, I see."

"Are you even paying any attention to me?" Lauren asked.

"Uh, not anymore," Justin admitted. "You lost me when you said mouth. That instantly got me thinking of yours and what it did to me just this morning."

Lauren blushed. She knew exactly what had happened between them that morning; they'd both been late to work. A fact that did not go unnoticed. The office chatterboxes had started speculating on the change in Lauren and Justin's relationship yesterday morning; now that it was Wednesday afternoon, the gossips were in overdrive.

"So," Justin teased as he bent over and lowered his lips to her left ear, "I've got a few minutes in between terribly boring meetings. I'm trying to get everything settled for Jared's return January 3, but nothing's more important than a stolen minute with you. Are you up for some sexual harassment from your boss?"

"My boss will get lipstick all over him," Lauren said as Justin's lips found her neck.

His left hand eased over her shoulder and slid beneath the vee of her shirt. "I didn't say you had to kiss the boss," he said between tantalizing nibbles.

"Oh," Lauren said. She tilted her neck to give Justin's lips better access. Did he have to smell so divine? And his hand… And when his lips touched her earlobe… "You know you're really driving me crazy and you should stop."

"Yes, I know." Regretfully, Justin straightened, his desire obvious. "It wouldn't look too professional of me to go into my meeting in this state. The clients are signing a huge contract, after all."

"Hmm," Lauren said with a nod. The sight of Justin's state had caused her mind to go blank.

"So what's tonight's schedule?"

"Hmm? Oh, I'm doing some shopping and going by the condo to grab some more things," Lauren said.

"Don't be too long," he leaned over and whispered in her ear.

"I'll be home around eight-thirty," Lauren said.

"Then I'll be waiting." He dropped a quick kiss on her lips and pulled back before he decided to linger. "You know I want to keep kissing you." He groaned. "I'll see you later."

"Bye," Lauren said. She stared through the open doorway, propped her elbow on her desk and rested her chin on her hand.

She wanted him, too.

Her phone buzzed. It was Trisha. "Yes?"

"Hi, Lauren. You've got that overseas call in two minutes. Also, Jeff called and wanted me to tell you that he'll be about five minutes late tonight."

"Thanks." Lauren frowned. Had she told Justin she was meeting Jeff? She couldn't remember, and now that he was going into a meeting it was too late. She'd tell him tonight, after she'd gotten everything straightened out with Jeff.

She planned to approach Justin with a clean conscience and recount exactly what she'd overheard. That way, she could put it behind her once and for all.

Her relationship with Justin could be the real thing.

She already loved him, a love different from the other time she'd thought she was in love. It wasn't puppy love. It wasn't infatuation. It wasn't being in love with the idea of love itself.

With Justin, she felt equal. Empowered. As though she'd met a partner who made her life more real, more fulfilling.

No doubt about it, she was in love with Justin Wright.

And even though he hadn't said the words, she had a feeling that he felt the same way. His actions told her every day.

It was beginning to look a lot like a very special Christmas.

JUSTIN GLANCED at his watch. A little after six-fifteen. It had been a long day at the office, but he'd accomplished a lot. In two days, he could leave knowing that Jared would come back to a job well done.

He'd taken a break earlier and strolled by Lauren's office around ten to five, but the dark interior indicated she'd already left. Now, as he put on his coat, he wondered what she was shopping for. He'd been wrangling with his own shopping dilemma for a couple of days now.

He wanted to give her an engagement ring for Christmas but that sounded so cliché. Besides, he'd told Lauren he'd take the relationship on her terms. She hadn't even said she loved him. Come to think of it, he hadn't said the words, either. Justin knew at that moment that he needed to start there.

So he decided to tell her tonight. Which of course brought him back to square one concerning the perfect Christmas present.

Then again, if he told her tonight, maybe by Christmas an engagement ring wouldn't seem so cliché. Maybe the permanent gift of his heart would be the best gift of all.

Gee, now he sounded like a greeting-card commercial. His mother cried every time she got one. Of course, she'd cry the minute Justin told her he was getting married, too.

He glanced at his watch again. Six-twenty. Time wasn't flying tonight and Lauren said she wasn't planning on being at his house until eight-thirty.

Maybe he should just go see Lauren now. Meet her

at her condo. That way he could follow her home, make sure she was okay. The temperature had dropped and that meant ice on the roads.

They could always get snowed in at her condo if worse came to worst. He flipped off his office light and headed for his car.

"SO, HOW ARE THINGS between you and my brother?" Jeff asked before putting a bite of baked chicken into his mouth. "You've been avoiding the question ever since I got here."

"I've been too busy cooking," Lauren said. "And somehow still doing your laundry."

"Yeah, I don't know what I'm going to do when you aren't living here anymore. Have you decided to sell the place or rent it?"

"That's still premature," Lauren said. The succulent Parmesan chicken in her mouth suddenly lost its flavor. "Justin and I still have quite a few things to work out."

Jeff hadn't lost his appetite and dug into the potatoes. "Like what? He's a great guy. You're a great guy—I mean gal." He saw her expression. "Oh, you know what I mean. So what's the problem?"

Lauren set her fork on the table. "There's a small matter of a conversation that I overheard at his house."

Jeff kept right on eating, indicating he didn't have the slightest clue what she was talking about. "What—was he on the phone with an ex or something? Some of them are pretty nasty."

Some of Jeff's were pretty nasty, as well, in Lauren's opinion, but she didn't bother to correct him. It was an irrelevant detail. "The conversation occurred when he was in the kitchen with you. I think the words you used were, 'Go for it.'"

"Oh." Jeff leaned back in his chair and looked at her. "That conversation."

"Yeah, that one. The one in his kitchen when I was sick. The one where you told Justin you didn't think he'd last a week with me. And then he said he would. Well, that's putting it nicely. It sounded more like a brotherly one-upmanship to me." Now that she'd gotten the words out, she felt a little better. She picked up her fork.

Jeff raked a hand through his hair. "That's what it was. Well, sort of. I was trying to convince him to ask you out. I know my brother, and I could tell that he liked you. But he's as stubborn as Jared. Both are mules when it comes to doing anything that might upset their orderly world. So I had to upset his world for him. That's what our conversation was about."

"Before this all happened with Justin, I thought I liked you."

Jeff nodded and picked his fork back up. "I figured as much. To tell you the truth, it made me a feel a little weird. I love you—don't get me wrong—but only as a friend. Hell, I can't wait to have you for a sister-in-law.

That will be the ultimate. I've never had a sister and you fit my brother so well. But as for there being an 'us' like in a you and me…."

"I know." Lauren shrugged. "I feel pretty foolish when I think that I wanted to make it more. I realize now that I was settling. Justin is safe and secure in an exciting way, and oh, does he make me simmer. No offense, but you don't."

"No offense taken," Jeff said. He finished his last bite, stood up and placed his empty plate in the sink. The timer on the washer beeped and he began moving things to the dryer. "Can I have these appliances when you take the plunge and totally move in with my brother? He's got a better set, anyway."

"Good grief," Lauren said.

Jeff started the dryer and grinned. "Don't say any more. I'm totally impossible. My mother thinks so, too. So, does Justin know that you overheard us talking?"

"No, but I'm going to tell him tonight. I have to admit that that conversation hurt. But it opened my eyes to what an idiot I'd been with you. Of course I started to doubt Justin. He seemed like Mr. Wonderful, but I didn't know the truth. Were his actions just a game to prove a point to you, or was what he felt real?"

"Do you still question that?"

"Oh, no. His feelings are real. I know it in my heart."

"So you love him."

"Absolutely." Lauren answered. She handed Jeff her

plate and he set it on the counter. "I'm still scared because I had one really bad experience."

"He's the same way," Jeff said. He sat back down. "He'll never talk about it, of course. But I don't know any guy who hasn't been burned at least once, and my brother is no exception. Not that he dwelled on whoever she is. It's just that after being burned, you think twice about trying again."

"Exactly. And he says we'll take this on my terms—nice and slow."

"That's great. Now, if I could only get my world worked out, all our lives might be fine."

Lauren frowned. Jeff was having problems? "You said you had something you wanted to talk to me about. What's going on?"

He grinned sheepishly. "Do you know Tori?"

"The girl in tech support. Sure. She was on the social committee. She said she liked working for you."

"Yeah, well." Jeff stood and leaned against the counter. "I don't know if she will anymore. I got together with her after the Christmas party. Her boyfriend had just dumped her, and she got terribly drunk. That's why I left you on the dance floor. I thought she was going to drive home."

"So did she?"

He shook his head. "No. I caught her in time, argued with her, got a hotel room, took her upstairs, made black coffee and—"

"I don't need all the details," Lauren said. Her face reddened as she remembered her own wondrous love-making with Justin. "So what's the problem? Can't she remember it?"

"Oh, she remembers it, all right. The next morning she woke up, kissed me, called it a mistake that we should put behind us and left. Yesterday I heard she was back with her ex."

"And you don't like that."

"Ah, hell, I don't know. I sure as hell didn't think I was simply a one-night stand to help her forget him. As for dating her, we work well together and both love computers. Is that really enough for a relationship?"

"Seems like she's really gotten under your skin," Lauren said.

"Maybe, but if she's back with Bozo, who am I to interfere? She's made what she wants clear. I have to respect her wishes. I was just a body to keep her warm that night."

"Ouch." He had a point.

Jeff glanced at his watch. "Tell you what: I'm going to get out of here. I'll dart over later and get the rest of this stuff. You okay to drive to Justin's? It's supposed to be icy out tonight."

"I'll be fine. I'll do these dishes, grab a few things and then go to Justin's." Lauren stood and put the glasses in the sink. "I'm ready to listen if you want to talk about Tori at any point."

"Thanks," Jeff said. "So, are you coming to Christmas? We're all headed to Branson, but I'm sure an emergency will pop up, or at least I hope so."

"I have no idea what we're doing. Justin hasn't asked me. My mother wants to go to Kansas City, so I might be headed there with her. I'll have my cell on. Call if you need me."

"Okay." Jeff held out his arms. "Come here and give me one last hug. If I know my brother, he's going to outlaw our hugs the moment he gets a ring on your finger, if not sooner."

"I'm my own person," Lauren said. She stepped into Jeff's embrace. He held her for a moment and put a kiss on the top of her head.

"You may be your own person, but if my brother loves you, he's going to be possessive. Not in a bad way or anything, but he can be insecure. A man in love always has doubts. He's always afraid that the best thing to happen to him will just up and vanish one day. Remember that."

"I will," Lauren said. She stepped out of Jeff's hug and shivered. "Does it feel cold in here to you?"

He frowned. "A bit, like you have a draft. Did you program your heat differently?"

"Justin did since I'm not here." Lauren went to check the thermostat. It read seventy degrees Fahrenheit. She tapped it and shrugged. "It looks fine. Must have just been a blast of cold air. It is getting windy out there and my windows aren't the best."

"You better get to Justin's before the weather gets any

worse," Jeff said. "Thanks again for dinner. I'm sure I'll be seeing you soon."

"I'm sure," Lauren said. She watched him leave and a sense of peace filled her. Tonight she'd talk to Justin and everything would finally be perfect.

She finished up and soon was on her way.

WHEN HE LEFT Lauren's condo, Justin didn't go home right away. Instead, he drove around aimlessly. He took the new Page Avenue extension into St. Charles County and then headed south on Highway 94. Eventually, he hit Highway 40, drove east, passed the Wright Solutions building and crossed the Daniel Boone Bridge into Chesterfield.

That he'd gone miles out of his way or made a complete circle didn't matter. He didn't care much about anything anymore. Seeing Lauren in Jeff's arms and seeing him put a kiss on the top of her head had been enough. Thank God he hadn't heard any lovey-dovey words, too.

He'd always wondered if he'd be one of those men who barged in, surprised the guilty couple and yelled a lot.

He'd just learned he wasn't. Instead, he had slipped right back out the door like a coward.

He drummed his fingers on the leather steering wheel. What did one do in this situation? He exited at Chesterfield Airport Road and wandered the slippery side roads until he hit Clarkson. From there it was north on Olive and a right turn on…

Her car was in the driveway when he finally pulled up. That surprised him. He'd wondered if once in Jeff's arms she wouldn't want to leave.

He didn't let the glimmer of hope dissuade him, though. He'd said that they'd take the relationship on her terms; however, if she wanted Jeff then there wasn't a relationship to begin with.

He'd promised that he'd do whatever made her happy, and if that meant Jeff… Yes, back to square one. Chivalry demanded he do the right thing, and the right thing was to let her go.

She rose from the couch the moment he was through the door, and held out her arms. "There you are! I just got home. I was so worried. You didn't answer your cell phone."

"I turned it off," Justin said. "Just me and the radio. No distractions."

Observing that he wasn't coming any closer, she dropped her arms to her sides. "Did you just leave work?"

His slipping out her unlocked front door had been successful. She and Jeff hadn't noticed his brief presence. "I left around six-thirty."

"Oh. Did you go do some Christmas shopping?"

"Something like that," Justin replied. He hated seeing the confusion on her beautiful face. He wanted to walk forward, reach out, gather her into his arms and plead with her to love him.

But her heart had never really been his, had it? She'd

never told him she loved him, and the fact still lurked that she'd wanted his brother enough to attempt a seduction. This evening, she hadn't even told Justin she was meeting Jeff. Not only had she met him, but she'd cooked him dinner. There was no way he could rationalize that Lauren and Jeff's evening had been a chance occurrence.

Jealousy had stripped from Justin the power to believe, to trust. Fate was not a kind bed mistress. He suddenly didn't feel like dealing with Lauren and her indiscretions. For better or worse, she was staying with him. "I'm going to call it a night."

She cocked her head and looked at him. "Are you okay? You aren't coming down with the flu, are you?"

No, he wasn't okay, and no, he wasn't catching her flu. She'd crawl into bed with him, sleep with him, give him her body, yet he'd never have her in the way that mattered. He'd never have her heart.

He couldn't live like that, but he'd sworn to her that he'd take their relationship on her terms. His predicament was unbearable.

"I'm fine," he answered. He shrugged out of his heavy winter coat and hung it up in the hall coat closet.

"Oh." She seemed totally lost. She clasped her hands. "By the way, I meant to tell you earlier that I met your brother before I came home. Later, when you feel better, can we talk?"

He didn't want to hear any explanations, any lies. "I'm really tired. Not tonight."

"Okay. Tomorrow, then."

"Tomorrow after work I'm headed straight to Branson. I've got to be there for Christmas—Christmas Eve service to attend, and some big family party beforehand. Unlike my brother, I won't be able to conjure up a reason not to go."

He winced. Damn. They'd never made plans, and now she appeared as if he'd slapped her. Her lower lip quivered. "Oh. Well, being with your family is important. My mother wants me to go to Kansas City."

"Yeah, right. Anyway, like I said, I'm sure Jeff will be around—he always has an excuse."

"I guess we should have talked Christmas plans before we started all this." Lauren gestured at all the Christmas decorations.

"Probably," Justin said. He moved into the kitchen and grabbed a bottle of beer from the fridge. A long cold one sounded like the ticket right now, and if nothing else, maybe it would help him get some much-needed sleep. Hell, he was too wound up to sleep.

Lauren followed him into the kitchen. He turned. Her hands were planted firmly on her hips. "Tell me what is going on."

He shrugged. He'd been so much of a Peeping Tom lately that he couldn't own up to it.

"What is this all about?" Lauren demanded.

When he didn't answer, she continued. "You don't want me anymore, do you? That's it. I can see by your downcast eyes that I'm right. You can't even face me. You won, didn't you? 'She won't reject me.' 'I'm not even going to bet on it—just rub your nose in it.' Do you remember all of that conversation you had with your brother, Justin Wright? Because I do. I remember every word. Jeff and I talked about it tonight. I didn't think I was wrong about you. I didn't think you meant it. I didn't think I was a game, a bet."

He glanced up then, and made the mistake of looking at her. Tears brimmed, and he knew his silence had inflicted pain. He hated himself. He had to let her go, for her sake and for his. If she loved Jeff, she had to be free. And he could not love her more each day without losing pieces of himself. Maybe this way would be best.

She shook her head as if turning her face from side to side would somehow give her understanding. "I was just a prize to you, revenge on your brother for that girl in college, wasn't I? That's all I was."

His anger—at her, at himself, at fate—made him lash back. "And I was just a substitute for Jeff."

She stared at him, her brown eyes widening in disbelief. "You are such a fool."

He was. He was about to watch the best thing that ever happened to him leave.

"This conversation is going nowhere." Lauren tossed

up her hands. "I'll get my stuff. You won. I didn't reject you. You can have your glory and your guts."

Her hands shook as she dug in her purse for her cell phone. She punched a speed-dial number and hit Send. "Hey," she said when the caller answered. "Will you go turn up my heat?" A pause. "Yes. I'm coming home."

There was another pause as Justin knew Jeff asked the obvious: "What's going on?" "I'll tell you later," Lauren said. She listened one moment more and snapped her phone shut. "Excuse me," she said to Justin.

Justin stepped aside. Then, as Lauren left the kitchen, he emptied the entire bottle of beer in the sink. He didn't want any of it. Did he need any other proof that he'd been right? She'd called Jeff. She was running to Jeff.

Oh, Justin hadn't meant any of those words Lauren had overheard, not literally. She wasn't a game, a bet. She was Lauren. He loved her.

But her heart belonged to someone else. To his twin brother, Jeff.

He heard the noise of a car engine as Lauren's car jumped to life, and said a quick prayer that she'd be safe on the roads.

And then, Justin Wright sat down on a kitchen chair, and for the first time in a long time, he let himself cry.

Chapter Thirteen

"Merry Christmas!"

"That's tomorrow, Mom," Jeff said. He leaned over and kissed his mother on the forehead. "Tonight's Christmas Eve."

Rose didn't look too concerned. "It's close enough. I'm just so happy! You and Justin are both here! Everyone I love and adore is in Branson. See how thrilled your father is?"

Jeff glanced into the family room, where his father sat with Uncle Melvin. "Dad's asleep in the easy chair."

"Well, never mind that. He's thrilled. So thrilled he can relax and sleep anywhere."

Jeff grinned. "Good try, Mom. Just remember that I'm here the next time you say I don't do anything for this family. I do a lot and, trust me, you're going to be thanking me over and over soon."

"What do you mean?

But Jeff stepped away from his mother. "Ah, here

comes Cousin Garrett and Grandmother. You're on this one. I think I'll find the food."

"Jeff!" his mother called.

"Just remember what I said. It'll all make sense later. I promise." Jeff strolled into the dining room, where the Wright family had set out enough food to feed a small army.

Of course, that was what seemed to be in the house. People Jeff didn't know or recognize filled every nook and cranny. Having purposely skipped all of these past joyous family events, he hadn't realized the Wright family Christmas Eve party was such a huge deal.

As he grabbed a piece of bacon candy, which was a bacon-wrapped chestnut dipped in brown sugar and broiled, he wondered how Lauren was faring. Hopefully, she was surviving her family events.

Her vacation hadn't started well. She'd come to his condo Wednesday night, told him what had happened between her and Justin, cried her eyes out, then gone home. He remembered the conversation as if it had just happened.

He wanted to kill his brother. What had the idiot been thinking?

Jeff reached for a wedge of turkey sandwich. His brother, giving up? That didn't make sense. "He said he was a substitute," Lauren had told Jeff. "He said he was wrong about me. But when I left work that night, everything was wonderful. When he came home, it was as if he'd done a complete turnaround."

Jeff chewed the sandwich and shivered. Someone had entered the house and brought a blast of cold air in with them.

Cold air. It was Jeff's job to track down solutions when there weren't any clues, his job to find answers when there weren't any obvious problems.

He'd just figured out what had happened that night at Lauren's. Leaving the food, Jeff went and discovered that his brother was in the living room, with their cousin Cindy. "We need to talk," he said.

"I am talking," Justin glibly replied. "Cindy is telling me about her reality-TV experiences. She's trying out for *Survivor* next."

"Yeah, I'll have to hear all about that later." Jeff smiled at his cousin. "I mean that seriously, Cindy. But not now. Pardon my rudeness, but will you excuse us? I really need to speak to my twin. *Now.*" Jeff placed his hand on his brother's elbow. "Let's go."

"Sure," Cindy said. She didn't seem to believe Jeff, but he didn't really care. He wouldn't come to Branson next year, anyway. Cindy, seeing Jeff was serious, shrugged and headed for the family room. "You two go have a good chat."

JUSTIN KNEW BETTER than to argue with Jeff in the midst of a family function. He could kick his brother's rear later, in private. He followed Jeff down a side hall, and once they were out of everyone else's hearing, he turned to his brother and said, "Okay, what's this sudden need to talk?"

"One word. Lauren. What did you do to her?"

"Do to her?" So forceful was Justin's sputter that if Justin had been drinking anything, he would have spit it out. "Why don't you ask her?"

"Oh, I did. You did a complete turnaround on her. She has no clue. She thinks it's all because of our conversation, that she was just a game to you."

"Yeah, right," Justin scoffed. "Lauren was never a game to me. Please. Try another one. In fact, I'll give *you* one. I just gave her what she wanted."

"And what was that?"

"You."

"Me?" To Justin's disgust, Jeff appeared shocked. "What are you talking about? She returned to her condo Wednesday night in tears. She was babbling something about our bet and that you really had meant it. Was that all Lauren was to you? Just a prize? Something you could win in revenge for Betty?"

Justin's head pounded and he shook it. "Did she ever tell you what happened between us?"

"What—at the hotel? About you two living together? No, Lauren didn't tell me about your sex life. Please, I don't want to know the gory details."

"That's not what I meant. I mean about the night she

changed her hair, showed up at your place all dolled up in nothing but a merry widow and a see-through robe, and started dancing? She was there with the intent of seducing you. Only, it was me lying on your couch, instead. Believe me, I learned right then how much Lauren wants you."

Jeff paused as he contemplated Justin's words. "No," he said slowly, "she didn't tell me about it. But that's irrelevant. Lauren's over her crush on me. She figured out that that's all it was—just a silly, girlish crush. She told me you made her burn. *Simmer* was the word she used. I don't do anything for her. And she knows that I can never have feelings for her, either. At least not like love ever after, death do us part. As a friend or a brother-in-law, yes, but nothing more."

Anger consumed Justin. "Tell me another one. You were wrapped all around her the other night at her place. I know. I saw you."

"I just figured that out," Jeff said. "That's why you and I are standing here talking. And for your information, nothing happened. She loves you, you idiot. You."

"It certainly didn't look that way."

"I gave her an innocent hug. And a kiss on the top of her head. I didn't touch her otherwise. And I'd just told her about my indiscretion with Tori."

Justin blinked. "Tori, from tech support?"

"Yes. Tori, from tech support," Jeff continued. "Lauren told me the night of the Christmas party that she needed to talk to me. What she wanted to talk about was having overheard our conversation at your house. She wanted to let me know she'd had a crush on me but that she'd realized it was silly. She felt pretty high-school-ish over it. Anyway, she was excited about starting a relationship with you and she wanted to put everything, which means me, behind her with a clear conscience. She might have had a crush on me at one point, but when she met you, she realized that what she felt for you was the real thing. Heck, even I won't cook her soup or baby her the way you did when she was ill."

"I'd do that for anyone."

"No, you wouldn't, and you know it. You've fallen for Lauren. She's everything you've ever wanted, and she loves you. Or at least, she did."

"I won't make her happy," Justin said. No way would he admit to his brother that he did love Lauren.

"Do I need to make you hit me like in the movie *Katrina*? You know, the classic about the two brothers and the chauffeur's daughter?"

"It's *Sabrina,*" Justin automatically corrected. "Once with William Holden, Humphrey Bogart and Audrey Hepburn, and then the modern Sidney Pollack version with Harrison Ford, Julia Ormond and Greg Kinnear."

Jeff threw his hands skyward. "See? You're a movie buff. So is she. This just proves that you two are perfect for each other."

Justin dug in. His heart was on the line, and it was

beating so hard that it was threatening to override his logic. "It doesn't prove anything."

"Yeah, it does. It also proves that you're a stupid, dumb fool."

Justin started to open his mouth.

"Don't even begin to say 'am not,'" Jeff said. "Just know that you broke her heart. No one else did but you. You had the chance for happiness and you threw it away. Just remember that when you're old and alone. You're the one who threw it all away."

And with that, Jeff walked off. Justin stared after him. Had he really thrown it all away? Because he loved Lauren more than life itself. He only wanted her happy.

Did she love him?

Was that possible?

Was he the only one who could make her happy?

If so, that made him an idiot. And if the shoe fit...

Now, what exactly was he going to do about it?

COUNTRY CLUB PLAZA in Kansas City twinkled with millions of bright lights, but despite the festiveness of all the stores, Lauren's heart wasn't into any Christmas cheer. Her aunt lived in one of the older houses just across the parkway from the plaza, and every inch of her aunt's home was packed with people, so Lauren had escaped upstairs to the guest bedroom she was sharing with her mother. She plopped down on the twin bed, leaned back and let her head fall on the pillow.

Some Christmas this was turning out to be. It was worse than the Christmas she'd broken up with Mike.

Despite everyone's well wishes and yuletide joy, even Santa himself couldn't cheer Lauren up this year. The one thing she'd wanted, the one thing she'd dreamed of, had slipped through her fingers.

She closed her eyes. Even in the darkness she could still see Justin's face. She could almost feel his lips on hers. She could almost smell him.

Her eyes flew open, but all that greeted her searching glance was an empty guest room. She sighed and leaned back again on the pillow.

She wanted to hate Justin Wright. Maybe that would help her feel better. She needed to despise him, be furious and angry.

Oddly, Lauren felt empty and hollow, instead. She'd lost her heart, and all the screaming in the world at how unfair it was that she'd fallen for an insensitive lout wouldn't do her any good. Now she had to pick herself up, dust herself off and go forward. She'd survived many life crises; she could survive this one, as well.

She did not need a man to make her complete.

She would let her heart heal; maybe eventually she'd love again. Eventually. The thought of loving again was a paradox; thinking of doing it made her stronger, thinking of doing it made her hurt.

She thought she'd found the man of her dreams. He'd

turned out to be exactly what she'd first thought of him: a cad. She should have trusted her first instinct.

"Lauren?" Lauren's mother slowly opened the door. "Hey. Are you feeling okay? Everyone's asking about you."

"I'm fine. Tell them I have a headache. Or that I drank too much eggnog," she said. "I *am* a flu victim. They'll believe it.

Her mother came and sat beside her. "Still hurting?"

"Oh, yeah," Lauren said. "But I tell myself it could be worse. I could have married him and then discovered what a horrible jerk he was."

"Now, now," her mother said. "You don't really mean that."

Lauren didn't, but saying the words gave her a false sense of empowerment. "Oh, come on. You're divorced. You know that men aren't all they are cracked up to be."

"No, some aren't," her mother said. "But your father was. And I loved him dearly. His death affected me a great deal, and I rebounded. I shouldn't have been so desperate to be with someone. I should have been able to stand on my own feet, to be alone. I paid dearly for that. I don't believe your situation with Justin is like that at all."

"I don't know what my situation is. One minute it was fine—the next he told me it was over. I have no idea what happened."

"Well, at least try to have some fun tonight. There are

so many people downstairs who haven't seen you in so long. And in thirty minutes we're going to head to the church for the midnight service."

"I'm planning on going to bed early."

"If you're sure that's what you want," her mother said. She leaned down and kissed Lauren's forehead. "I'll check on you later."

"Thanks." Lauren waited until her mother had left before grabbing her night things and getting ready for bed. As Christmas Eve turned into Christmas, Lauren fell fast asleep.

THE SMELL OF BACON woke her up the next morning, and around 10:00 a.m., she got up, showered and made her way downstairs. Her aunt and uncle were already up and about.

"Hi, Aunt Gail, Uncle Kyle," she said as she entered the kitchen.

"Good morning to you, too," Aunt Gail said. She dropped some strips of cooked bacon on a paper-towel-covered plate. "Hungry?"

"Not really," Lauren said as she settled on a bar stool at the island. Her aunt wore a loud Christmas apron with a big reindeer face on it. Lauren herself had dressed simply, in her red fitted sweater and a pair of black pleated pants. "What time is everyone arriving for the festivities?"

"Around noon for brunch," Aunt Gail said. "Is your mother awake yet?"

Lauren shook her head. "No."

Aunt Gail waved her spatula. "Your mother always was a night owl. When we were kids, she always partied until the cows came home." The doorbell sounded and Aunt Gail frowned. "Now, who can that be this early?"

Uncle Kyle helped himself to another serving of scrambled eggs. "I don't know. Doesn't the postal service guarantee delivery of express-mail packages even on Christmas Day?"

"We have all our packages," Aunt Gail said. "That would be pretty impressive for the postal service, though. It snowed last night and we got another two inches."

"Great. I'll have to shovel again before everyone arrives," Kyle said.

The doorbell shrilled again. Gail wiped her hands on her apron. "I'll go see who it is. Lauren, make sure the bacon doesn't burn. Your uncle can't cook a thing. At least he can shovel."

Lauren climbed off the bar stool and walked around the island. Her aunt's kitchen was huge and contained every gourmet amenity. Lauren picked up a spatula.

"Slide more of those over here," Uncle Kyle said as Lauren fished some cooked bacon out of the skillet. "Christmas is my one and only day I get to go off my bland and boring diet and eat all the high-cholesterol things the doctor and my wife say are bad for me."

"Well, have at," Lauren said as she pushed the plate over. "You enjoy it."

"Oh, I will," Kyle said. Lauren watched him crunch into a piece of bacon. Kyle stood six foot six and was as thin as Abraham Lincoln had been. Yet at age sixty he'd had one heart attack and skyrocketing cholesterol that had to be lowered. Looks could certainly be deceiving.

"So who was it?" Kyle asked as Gail reentered the room.

"You were right. It was a package. It's for Lauren. I left it in the living room. It's huge."

"Huge?" Kyle's eyes widened. "What would someone have sent here for you? Hmm. I wonder if my sister came up with something. Do you remember, Gail, the year she had tropical flowers delivered?"

"I remember," she said. "They filled almost every room in the house. She certainly went overboard."

"So, Lauren, what did you ask for?" Kyle asked.

"I don't know," Lauren said. "I don't remember asking my mother for anything specific. I guess I'll find out later."

Aunt Gail turned off the heat under the skillet. "Oh, posh. Go take a peek now and come back and tell us what you think it might be. I'm dying of curiosity. It barely made it in the door."

"Okay," Lauren said. She stood up. "I'll be right back."

The trip through the dining room took only a few seconds. When Lauren crossed the foyer and stepped into the living room, she paused.

Nothing seemed any different from yesterday evening. As for some big, huge package, Aunt Gail must have been hallucinating. All the packages under the tree looked as if they had easily made it through the door.

"Aunt Gail, what are you talking about? There's nothing in here."

"Sure there is," Gail called back. "You just need to look harder."

Lauren surveyed the room one more time and then turned around. She heard the powder-room toilet flush, but that didn't provide any clue. "Aunt Gail, do me a favor. Get in here and tell me what I'm missing."

"Hopefully, you're missing me."

Lauren jumped as the familiar baritone voice washed over her. Her hands flew to her cheeks.

"Shh, calm. You always do that. It's just me."

Striding toward her was the man to whom the voice belonged. Justin Wright. Her aunt's words made sense now. A large package that barely got in the door. But he'd made it past her aunt's defense system. "What are you doing here?"

"Merry Christmas," he said.

"Merry Christmas," Lauren replied stiffly. "You haven't answered my question."

"I came because I need to see you, talk to you. I've recently realized that I've been a complete idiot."

"It took thirty years for you to figure that out?"

Justin winced. "I guess I deserve that."

"That and a lot more," Lauren said. "So what am I now—an excuse for you to get out of Branson?"

"No, I don't need an excuse. Do you really think I drove through a snowstorm all night just to get away from my relatives? Even Jeff's still there."

"So why are you here, then?"

"I told you—I came to see you."

"You made it clear to me on Wednesday that there was no point in seeing me."

"You don't make it easy on a guy, do you? Should I get down on my knees and grovel first?"

She eyed him suspiciously. The usually impeccable Justin Wright looked a mess. He hadn't shaved; his clothes were wrinkled as if he'd slept in them or sat in them all night. "Did you even go to Branson?" she asked.

"Yep, and while there got a tongue-lashing from my brother on the error of my ways. You can call him if you don't believe me. So, I drove up here to tell you I was wrong."

"I'm not taking you back," Lauren said.

"And I don't blame you," Justin said. "But for closure, then, at least hear me out."

She should at least do that. "Okay."

He shifted his feet. "I went to your condo that night and saw you with Jeff. I jumped to the wrong conclusion. I left and went home, and when you came back that night, I reacted." Justin stopped.

"That's it?" Lauren's mouth slowly dropped open.

"You saw me in an innocent hug with your brother and you broke up with me? I don't believe you could be so, so idiotic!"

Justin grinned wryly. "Trust me, now I feel about the same way. I should have trusted you and, instead, I let my jealousy get in the way. You'd always wanted Jeff. You two get along perfectly, it seems. How could I be the better man for you? All I could do is love you."

"Love me?"

"Love you," Justin said. "I love you so much that it hurts when I'm not with you. I love you so much that if Jeff is the man you want, well, I thought I was doing the chivalrous thing and setting you free so that you could be with him."

She stared at him. He loved her? "You didn't ask me what I wanted."

"No. I just saw you with him and I jumped to the wrong conclusion. I've been doing a lot of that lately. You hadn't told me you were meeting him."

Jeff's words came back to haunt Lauren: "A man in love always has doubts. Remember that."

"No, I didn't tell you," Lauren admitted. "I forgot and then you went into your meeting and then I planned to tell you when I got home. I wanted to set things straight with Jeff. I wanted to ask him about that conversation. I wanted some perspective before I came home that night."

"He told me all this. He filled me in." Justin again

shifted his weight from foot to foot, a sure sign he was nervous. "I always told you our relationship was on your terms. You wanted slow. When I saw you with Jeff…"

He raked a hand through his hair. "I guess I'm just here to apologize and tell you I'm sorry. I never meant to hurt you. I can see now that my words when you came home were really cruel. I just wanted you to be happy, and if it was with Jeff…"

Her lips trembled. "I wanted you."

He looked at her and her heart broke. "I know that now."

"I still want you," Lauren said, and as the words left her lips she knew that no truer words had been spoken. "You see, I think I fell for you that night when I kissed you and realized you weren't your brother. You made me feel things no other man has ever made me feel. Passion, tenderness, joy. And happy. I felt happy. Not right away, of course, but later, I found myself realizing that you were everything I wanted. With you I feel I can do anything, be anything. Not that I'm incomplete without you, but somehow you make me even better. You see, I love you, Justin Wright. Wholly. Without restraint. And your words that night hurt. When you talked to Jeff, you said you'd keep me for a week. You talked about me as though I was a prize, something to be won. Not something to be partnered, or cherished, or loved."

"I was wrong," he whispered.

"You were," Lauren said. "But luckily for you, today

is Christmas and Christmas is the time of giving. That means I'm going to give you one more chance. Just one. Even Scrooge got another chance."

"He did," Justin said. "He was a changed man."

"Are you a changed man?"

Justin shook his head. "No."

She tilted her chin and looked up at him. *"No?"*

"No. You see, I can't change the fact that I love you with all my heart. And I did mean it when I said that I'd keep you for a week. However, what I didn't tell my dimwit brother or you was that I planned on keeping you forever. You see, I can have this relationship on your terms, as long as you understand mine. My terms are forever. I love you, and I'm going to be the only man to love you for the rest of your days."

A thrill shot through Lauren. "And what does this mean?"

"It means marriage, kids, the whole thing. But only with you. And only when you're ready. I wanted to buy you an engagement ring for Christmas, but thought that might be too forward of me, even a bit cliché. I hadn't even told you I loved you yet."

Lauren nodded. "Yeah. It might have been premature. But Valentine's Day might be about right. Until then, you already gave me a heart to wear."

He took her hand and placed it on his chest. "And I give you my real heart. It's yours, Lauren. I love you."

Lauren smiled and held out her other arm to him. Justin wrapped her arms around him and enveloped her in a giant hug. He leaned his head down, and when their lips touched, they shared a long, passionate kiss before some discreet coughing had them pulling slightly apart. They still kept their arms around each other as they turned to face Lauren's aunt, uncle and her mother.

"So, did I do okay letting him in the door? I almost didn't, you know," her aunt said.

"You did," Lauren said. "He's the best gift I could ever have."

She faced the man of her dreams, the man she would marry and spend the rest of her life with. "I love you," she said.

He touched the tip of his finger to her nose. His smile lit up his whole face and Lauren knew that every single word he uttered next was true—and always would be. "And I love you right back."

AMERICAN Romance®

Catch the latest story in
the bestselling miniseries by

Tina Leonard

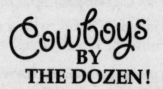

Cowboys BY **THE DOZEN!**

The only vow Calhoun Jefferson will take is to stay
away from women, children, dogs and shenanigans.
He knows all too well what happens to a man who
gets into hijinks—a trip to the altar! But when rodeo
queen Olivia Spinlove gallops into town, Calhoun
may reconsider the appeal of a family adventure—
especially if her two matchmaking kids have
anything to say about it!

CATCHING CALHOUN
by Tina Leonard
Book #1045

Available December 2004!

And don't miss—

ARCHER'S ANGELS
Coming in February 2005!

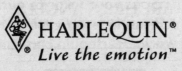

If you enjoyed what you just read,
then we've got an offer you can't resist!

Take 2 bestselling love stories FREE!

Plus get a FREE surprise gift!

Clip this page and mail it to Harlequin Reader Service®

IN U.S.A.	IN CANADA
3010 Walden Ave.	P.O. Box 609
P.O. Box 1867	Fort Erie, Ontario
Buffalo, N.Y. 14240-1867	L2A 5X3

YES! Please send me 2 free Harlequin American Romance® novels and my free surprise gift. After receiving them, if I don't wish to receive anymore, I can return the shipping statement marked cancel. If I don't cancel, I will receive 4 brand-new novels every month, before they're available in stores! In the U.S.A., bill me at the bargain price of $4.24 plus 25¢ shipping & handling per book and applicable sales tax, if any*. In Canada, bill me at the bargain price of $4.99 plus 25¢ shipping & handling per book and applicable taxes**. That's the complete price and a savings of at least 10% off the cover prices—what a great deal! I understand that accepting the 2 free books and gift places me under no obligation ever to buy any books. I can always return a shipment and cancel at any time. Even if I never buy another book from Harlequin, the 2 free books and gift are mine to keep forever.

154 HDN DZ7S
354 HDN DZ7T

Name	(PLEASE PRINT)	
Address	Apt.#	
City	State/Prov.	Zip/Postal Code

Not valid to current Harlequin American Romance® subscribers.

Want to try two free books from another series?
Call 1-800-873-8635 or visit www.morefreebooks.com.

* Terms and prices subject to change without notice. Sales tax applicable in N.Y.
** Canadian residents will be charged applicable provincial taxes and GST.
   All orders subject to approval. Offer limited to one per household.
   ® are registered trademarks owned and used by the trademark owner and or its licensee.

AMER04R   ©2004 Harlequin Enterprises Limited

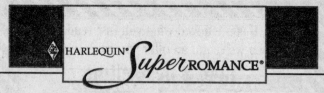

HARLEQUIN *Super*ROMANCE®

A six-book series from Harlequin Superromance.

WOMEN in Blue

Six female cops battling crime and corruption on the streets of Houston. Together they can fight the blue wall of silence. But divided, will they fall?

Coming in December 2004,
The Witness by Linda Style
(Harlequin Superromance #1243)

She had vowed never to return to Houston's crime-riddled east end. But Detective Crista Santiago's promotion to the Chicano Squad put her right back in the violence of the barrio. Overcoming demons from her past, and with somebody in the department who wants her gone, she must race the clock to find out who shot Alex Del Rio's daughter.

Coming in January 2005,
Her Little Secret by Anna Adams
(Harlequin Superromance #1248)

Abby Carlton was willing to give up her career for Thomas Riley, but then she realized she'd always come second to his duty to his country. She went home and rejoined the police force, aware that her pursuit of love had left a black mark on her file. Now Thomas is back, needing help only she can give.

Also in the series:
The Partner by Kay David (#1230, October 2004)
The Children's Cop by Sherry Lewis (#1237, November 2004)

And watch for:
She Walks the Line by Roz Denny Fox (#1254, February 2005)
A Mother's Vow by K.N. Casper (#1260, March 2005)

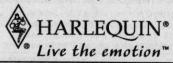

◆ HARLEQUIN®
Live the emotion™

HSRWOMIB1204

AMERICAN *Romance*®

A COWBOY AND A KISS
by Dianne Castell

Sunny Kelly wants to save the old saloon
that her aunt left her in a small Texas town.

But Sunny isn't really Sunny.
She's Sophie Addison, a Reno attorney,
and she's got amnesia.

That's not about to stop cowboy
Gray McBride, who's running hard for
mayor on a promise to clean up the town—
until he runs into some mighty strong
feelings for the gorgeous blonde.

*On sale starting December 2004—
wherever Harlequin books are sold.*

HARLEQUIN®

AMERICAN *Romance*®

Baby
to be

**A Baby to Be is always
something special!**

SANTA BABY
by Laura Marie Altom
(November 2004)

Christmas Eve. Alaska. A small-plane crash—
and nine months later, a baby. But Whitney and
her pilot, Colby, are completely at odds about
their son's future. Until the next Christmas!

THE BABY'S
BODYGUARD
by Jacqueline Diamond
(December 2004)

Security expert Jack Arnett and his wife, Casey,
are getting divorced because she wants children
and he doesn't. But—and Jack doesn't know this—
Casey's already pregnant with his child....